The Broken Glass Mystery

A Duke Moran Novel

by Don Monroe

DORRANCE
PUBLISHING CO
EST. 1920
PITTSBURGH, PENNSYLVANIA 15238

Dorrance Publishing Co
585 Alpha Drive
Pittsburgh, PA 15238
Visit our website at *www.dorrancebookstore.com*

ISBN: 978-1-6491-3511-7
eISBN: 978-1-6491-3928-3

Chapter 1

. . . .

June 8, 1993 Saturday 11:00 p.m.

Anna had just fallen asleep in bed with a book lying in her lap. She was awakened by the sound of what she thought sounded like glass breaking. She wasn't sure if it was a dream, so she just lay there listening. It was so quiet in the house she could hear her heart beating. She tried to slow her breathing and relax so she could hear any unusual sounds in the house. Her husband George lay next to her, gently snoring.

Then all of a sudden, she heard some noises coming from the downstairs and she tensed up. It sounded like there was someone moving around down there.

She then nudged George to wake him up. She shushed him up when he started to mumble, and whispered to him that she heard some noises downstairs. He listened and could hear some noises also. So he sat up and at the same time reached into his nightstand for his pistol. It wasn't something he wanted to use unless he absolutely had to. He only shot it once a year at the range, but at close range he could hit his target.

The house was completely dark and all you could hear were the normal sounds you usually hear at night. You know, such as the various ticks and creaks that old houses make. But George didn't hear the other sounds such as the refrigerator or air-conditioning humming or rattling. It reminded George of the solar eclipse that just occurred about a month ago. Even the insects were silent for that. George figured the electricity had been turned off.

He whispered to Anna to call 9-1-1 and stay in the bedroom. Anna just sat there frozen from fear. George shook her and told her again to call the police. Then she finally came to her senses and fumbled around for the phone.

Their home was an older two-story colonial. But they had remodeled the whole house when they bought it. George slowly crept his way down the stairs and thought he'd head for the kitchen first. When he got to the bottom of the stairs, he had the strong feeling someone else was in the room with him. It was a moonless night, so he had to feel his way around the corner at the bottom of the steps. He started to turn and head for the kitchen when all of a sudden, he heard a squeak to the left. He quickly turned his head that way. Next thing he knew the whole world started going dark.

Upstairs Anna finally found the phone and started to dial when she heard the bedroom door start to open. She thought it odd that George would be back so soon and not letting her know it was him.

She saw a dark figure come through the door and come towards her. She spoke softly asking, "George, is everything all right?"

All of a sudden there was a sharp pain in her chest and everything went black as she passed out.

Chapter 2

. . . .

Saturday Evening 12:30 p.m.

I was in the middle of a really good dream when I was awoken by the sound of what sounded like breaking glass. I wasn't sure if I dreamt it or if it was real. The house was deadly silent and pitch black. I couldn't see my hand in front of my face. The electricity must be off because my digital clock is dark and the night light in the hallway is off. I like it dark when I sleep, so I have room darkening shades on the windows. I hear some noises downstairs and what sounds like more breaking glass. I roll out of bed and at the same time reach under the bed for the Louisville Slugger bat I found when cleaning out this old house. I do have a pistol, but it's in a lock box in the closet and it's not loaded. I never figured on needing it again.

My name is Duke Moran, and yes, I was named after John Wayne. My dad loved to watch westerns. I never figured out how he saw so many because they used to only get two channels on their television sets back then. I'm sure he must have gone to the movie theater a lot back then. What else did they have to do except work. Maybe I should say work, sex, or go to the movies.

I bought this place about three years ago at a courthouse tax auction. It had been empty for about five years, so I had a lot of refurbishing to do. Well, that's a story for later, and I know you're waiting for me to get my butt downstairs to see what's going on.

It's a big old house with two stairways to the second floor. There's one at each end of the house. The closest to me goes down to the living room. The other stairway on the far side of the house goes down to the kitchen. I figured the glass breaking was probably from the back door, which is in the kitchen. So, I decided to go down the living room stairway. That way I wouldn't be exposed at the bottom if someone is in the kitchen. The stairway is carpeted, so it masks my footsteps going down. I try stepping on the sides of each step to hopefully eliminate any creaking. I think I read about that in some mystery novel a long time ago.

So here I am sneaking down the steps hoping my bones aren't rattling from fear. I shouldn't be scared after spending a year in the jungles of Vietnam and being in firefights day and night. But it's different when you're all alone and with no one near you covering your back. Over in Nam you were scared, but you also knew that there was a bunch of your buddy's right there with you.

I did remember to grab a flashlight off the dresser on my way out of the bedroom. But I don't want to use it and expose my position just yet plus it would ruin my night vision.

I get to the bottom of the stairs and all is quiet so far. I sneak through the living room going towards the kitchen. When I get to the doorway, I peek inside and I see nothing. So, I go to the back door and can see one of the panes of glass is broken out. I decide to turn on the flashlight to check out the porch. It looks all clear, but I notice that there's broken glass on the porch floor. This is strange because it means the pane was broken from the inside out. You wouldn't break the glass to get out with the lock on the inside of the door. It doesn't make sense, so I figure I'd better check the rest of the house out and double check all windows and doors.

You probably wonder why I don't call the cops instead of checking things out myself. First of all, I figure that with my combat experience I should be able to handle just about anything. But mainly I had some trouble with the law last night and probably wouldn't get much cooperation from them.

Chapter 3

. . . .

I live in a small town in northern Wisconsin called Black Crow. The police force is pretty much a family affair as the police chief is the father of two of the patrolmen, uncle of a third, and brother of our only detective.

I stopped last night at the Boars Head Bar, which is the local hot spot in town. After a few beers, I struck up a conversation with a beautiful young lady sitting by herself at the bar. Her name was Jesse and she was a teacher from Black River Falls, which is about seventy miles from us. The school was on spring break, and she came over to visit her folks who lived on the lake.

We talked for about an hour when up walks Rick Turner, who happens to be the police chief's youngest son. He's the only one that's not on the police force. Rick is what you would call a spoiled brat and is definitely a bully. But he's not very big and was always protected by his older brothers. I didn't see his brothers anywhere around here in the bar.

He came up to me and started getting pushy and saying I was hitting on his date. I mentioned that most men don't leave a date sitting by themselves at the bar for an hour. He then told me, and not very politely, that I'd better get lost.

He said, "My dad's the police chief here, and all it takes is a phone call from me. He doesn't like troublemakers in his town."

I in turn replied, "Why don't you grow up and take care of your own problems? I'm sure your dad is too busy to babysit you."

This really set him off, and he took a step towards me and started swinging. I let him hit me once and warned him to stop. He kept coming, so I gave him a quick left to the head and a right to the gut. He went down for the count. He's not very tough except for his mouth, and I guess he thought I'd be a pushover.

Anyways a police officer shows up, and it was a new rookie that had just joined the police force. The manager must have called the cops. So the rookie, not knowing who Rick was, arrested the both of us. He threw both of us in the back seat of the squad car. I wouldn't be surprised if he loses his job for taking Rick into the station. Rick gave him plenty of backtalk all the way to the station. He made all kinds of threats at him, but the rookie took it all in stride.

At the station we were put in two separate cells. Then shortly after that, Rick's dad (the police chief) must have shown up. I figured I was going to be sitting in this cell forever, seeing whose son I decked. They took Rick out first and I don't know where they took him, but about a half hour later they came and got me. They took me up to the front to an interrogation room, and then I sat there for another half hour.

Finally, John Turner, the police chief himself, comes in and asks me what happened. Now Big John stands about six foot six and weighs in at around two fifty, so I know better than to give him any backtalk. I told him the truth about what happened and I think he believed me, but I think he had to side with his son. So basically, he chewed me out and told me not to show back up here again. I didn't argue and was happy to get away so easily. I didn't even ask about a ride back to my place. I figured I could walk the mile and a half.

Chapter 4

. . . .

So back to my immediate problem in my house. After checking the porch, I figure I'd better go to the basement next to check the fuse box. I still have fuses because I haven't gotten around to switching over to circuit breakers yet. Going into the dark basement in the middle of the night doesn't sound like a lot of fun. I know it sounds weird, but I felt safer in the jungles of Vietnam. At least there you weren't boxed in with walls. There might have been Viet Cong all around you, but we always found a way out. Well, I have to admit, there were a couple of times we were pinned down and didn't think we'd make it out. But I'm happy to say I'm here today.

The flashlight is starting to dim somewhat, and I know there's no fresh batteries for it in the house. So I figure I'd better get my ass in gear and get down there.

The door for the basement is in the kitchen, so I go to it and start to turn the knob. Of course, it has to squeak and the door creaks as I open it. And it sounds ten times louder than it is because of the dead quiet in the house. If anyone is down there, they sure as hell know I'm coming. I take a deep breath and start down the stairs.

If you've ever been in the basement of an old house you know there are a lot of dark places to hide, even if the lights are working. I get to the bottom and have to walk around the old octopus furnace to get to the other side where the fuse box is. The old fuse box has a lever on one side to turn the electricity on and off. The lever is in the down position, meaning it was shut off. There's no way it can shut off accidentally because it takes quite a bit of force to move it. I reach up and push the lever up and instantly the house goes from complete silence to being alive. You hear clicking sounds and the humming of the refrigerator all at once.

Of course, I forgot to turn on the light switch for the basement when I came down, so I'm still in darkness. I cross the basement and head up the stairs. At the top I turn on the lights and go back down to make sure the basement is clear. When I'm down there I get a funny feeling like I'm being watched or that someone has been here. You know that feeling where it feels like the hair is standing up on the back of your neck. I find no one down there and everything looks good, so I go back upstairs.

I check out the rest of the house and everything is fine, and I see no sign of anyone being in here. I notice its four thirty in morning, so I guess I won't get any more sleep tonight. I go out to the garage, where I have a temporary workshop set up. I find some glass and cut it down to fit the window pane. I get it put it in and all caulked up and everything cleaned up by about six thirty. So, I figure I might just as well go get some breakfast.

Chapter 5

. . . .

June 9 Sunday Morning

I went downtown to our only restaurant in our town, Barb's Diner. I found my best friend Eddy Jones sitting in a booth by the windows. I joined him and as I sat down, Janice the waitress, came right over. She said she was surprised to see me after last night, as she was also at the Boars Head Bar. She thought as I did last night that I'd be locked up for a while. I told her I was as surprised myself, but happy to be out.

I ordered some bacon, eggs, hash browns, and toast for breakfast. Eddy asked what happened last night, so I told him the whole story. He was shocked that I was let go so easy too. The police chief can be pretty tough on anyone messing with his family.

Eddy is the only person I really trust in this town. He is the only person that has a key to my house. I frequently take off fishing, sometimes for days at a time. When this happens, Eddy gets my mail and checks on the house for me. I tell Eddy what happened at my house last night or should I say this morning. He's as confused as I am about the strange happenings. He gets his keys out and shows me that he still has my key. He has been gone all night down in Madison working on an air-conditioning unit at one of the stores his company owns. He's just getting back now and heading home to bed.

Our food comes, so we dig in and eat. You've probably noticed that most guys don't spend a lot of time talking when there's food on the table. Especially when the food is as good as this. It's hard to find food as good as Barb's.

When we're finished, we make small talk for a while. In walks Jerry Kline, another fishing friend of ours. He comes over and sits with us and asks if we heard the big news from last night. I said, "Do you mean about me getting arrested last night?"

He replies, "No, I didn't hear about that." So I told the story again.

Then he told us what he had heard. Apparently, last night, there was a house broken into and the people murdered and robbed. It was a very well to do, retired couple from Illinois. They had bought the old Anderson house a year ago. As far as the cops can tell, a lot of jewelry was taken and an undetermined amount of cash. And as far as he knew, nobody had been arrested yet.

A murder and robbery are something that just doesn't happen around here. If the cops are smart, they'll call in help from the state police or Black River Falls police. I should know, I used to be a detective on the Madison police force.

We spend the next half an hour talking about the murder and wondering whether it could be a local person that did it or some outsider. Since we didn't know any facts about the case, there wasn't much we could figure out. It did seem that everyone in the diner was talking about the killings.

We ordered another cup of coffee just as Jimmy Woods walked in. Jimmy works at Ricks Feed and Grain. It's a local feed mill that gets corn, beans, and other crops for storage from the local farmers. They also grind up and bag feed for sale there, and they also deliver.

Jimmy came over to our table to join us. He said he heard about the murder last night so we didn't have to rehash that. But he said he had the weirdest thing happen to him yesterday.

Jimmy makes most of the deliveries of bulk feed to the smaller farmers in our area. He's been driving the same feed truck for years and has driven on just about every country road within fifty miles.

Well, Jimmy said, "Yesterday I had a delivery to make out on old Pothole Road, which is west of here." Pothole is not the real name of the road. It's actually Porter Road, but it's so rough that everyone calls it Pothole Road. You can tear up a set of tires and rims driving too fast on that road.

"There's an old railroad trestle that runs overhead about three miles out. What with the road being so rough and in need of repaving along there, I have to slow down or risk hitting my head on the headliner from bouncing up and down. I was doing about ten miles an hour when I entered under the trestle.

Next thing I know there's a bang with a screeching sound, and I'm thrown forward toward the steering wheel. Luckily I had on my seat belt and it stopped me before I ate the steering wheel."

"There I sat with the top of the truck jammed under the trestle. I've driven under that trestle hundreds of times in the last five years with the same truck and never had any problems. I got out of the truck, but not without some pain in my chest. The seat belt did some damage but probably saved my face. It didn't look like I was jammed in super tight."

"I tried to back the truck out from under, but it wouldn't budge. I even had the tires spinning. So, I get back out to check out what to do next. I had to get it out from under there somehow. I then get a brainy idea."

"I let some air out of the tires, which enabled me to back the truck out. I then turned around and headed back to the mill. Back at the mill I went to Rick's office and told him what happened. I said I couldn't see the trestle sinking lower, or how the truck suddenly got higher."

"Come to find out Rick had new tires put on the truck last week on my day off, and he forgot to tell me. He called the service station where he had the tires installed. Jack, the owner of the shop said there had been a service notice put out that the size tire the truck used had been discontinued. The replacement they recommended was narrower but had higher side walls. It added about two and a half inches to the total height."

Apparently, that was enough to allow the truck to hit the train trestle. We all got a good laugh about what happened, but were happy that Jimmy was okay.

Jimmy said the worst thing now was that he would have to drive about five miles out of his way for that delivery from now on. And he said he would start watching overheads a lot more.

Chapter 6

. . . .

I headed home to work on the upstairs bathroom I'm remodeling. It's taken me three years to get the kitchen, downstairs bathroom, and one bedroom done. I don't have a regular job anymore, because I inherited a pile of money from a long-lost uncle.

The Moran family came over from Germany after the war and most settled in New York. A few spread out through the states. I had an uncle Morty, he was my father's brother. He stayed in New York and opened a small restaurant. Over the years he opened several more all over the city and state of New York. He also invested in real estate. He had at one time owned the land that the twin towers were built on.

Anyways when he passed, he left everything to me. He never had any kids and my father and he were very close. I remember that he used to send me money on my birthdays and Christmas. After his passing, I went to New York and sold off all the property, or at least got a realtor working on it. It was unbelievable how much property he still owned. It took about three years to get everything sold off.

So, I actually don't need to work, but I don't like to just sit around. I need to keep busy. That's one reason I bought this old house. It's nice to be able to work on these projects at one's leisure.

I started painting on the last wall in the upstairs bathroom, which is all I had left to do in there. I heard a car pull into the driveway, so I took a look out the window to see who is here. It's a police car, and I see Chief Turner getting out of it. He knocks on the front door so I go down to see him. He's a lot friendlier to me today which makes me suspicious. He asks if he can have a few words with me. And then he informs me I did nothing wrong. I ask if we can talk upstairs so I can finish the wall I'm painting so my paint brush and roller don't dry out on me. He says that's fine, so we head on up there.

The chief tells me there was a murder last night, and that was why he happened to be at the station house last night. I told him I had heard that this morning and that he'd have his hands full with that investigation. He admitted it was going to be tough and that he had no experience in running a murder investigation. He also said no one on the force had any experience either. There had never been a murder in our town or the area that anyone could remember.

The police department actually covers three towns and three lakes. The whole area is only about thirty miles in diameter. Black Crow is the biggest town with around twelve hundred people with Heron Lake wrapped partially around it. Then there's the town of Chaney with Crabs Lake, and the town of Rosewood with Willow Lake. The lakes all have a lot of summer homes, with most of the people either retired or coming up from Illinois. It keeps pretty busy in the area during the summer and nice and quiet during the winter.

So Chief Turner finally gets to why he's here. He says, "Duke, I'd like to hire you to lead the investigation. You've had experience in police work, and I know you helped solve two cases of murder in Madison. You would have total control and the assistance of the whole department."

I'm totally shocked and got out of police work because there are too many rules and laws protecting the guilty people. It really handcuffs the police in doing their jobs. The chief is practically begging me to do the job, and says they'll give me a car and anything else I need. He did say that he couldn't afford a lot of money with the budget they have. I tell him to just pay me what they pay the one detective on the force minus benefits. I have insurance and don't need vacation time. He agreed to those terms if I take the job. I did say that this is just temporary until the case is solved.

I finally agree to look into it and want to start with a look at the murder scene. He says he'll take me there right away if I'm ready. So I clean my paint brush out and change into some decent clothes. We then head out to his car and take off for the murder scene. He said he would cover what they knew as we go through the Anderson house. He did say there are two dead adults and they had both stabbed multiple times.

Chapter 7

. . . .

We arrive at the Anderson home, which is across town (Black Crow) from my place. The house is a decent size two-story house with a single-car garage in the rear. The house is in excellent shape, looking like it was just painted. It also has a full open front porch for relaxing in the evenings. I think seventy-five percent of the houses in our town have front porches.

We enter through the front door when we get there. I ask the chief if the crime scene has been processed at all. He says he had his brother Rob, who is the police forces only detective, go in and take pictures and dust for finger-prints. I really doubt that was done very thorough.

The chief showed me where George Anderson's body was found. It was at the bottom of the stairs, and there was a lot of blood still left there drying on the floor. There were bloody footprints going up the stairs. But upon closer examination you couldn't see any shoe or boot tread. They were smooth, meaning the assailant must have been in socks or wearing those foot covers like they have at the hospital.

The chief says, "It looks like Mr. Anderson must have been taken by surprise and stabbed multiple times. He never got a shot off with the pistol that we figured was his. It was lying next to his body."

"The electricity was turned off when the officers got here. So, we figure Mr. Anderson was probably blindsided when he came downstairs."

We then headed upstairs to check out the bedroom where Mrs. Anderson had been killed.

"Apparently Anna Anderson had been stabbed to death in her bed. We went upstairs to the master bedroom and found her dead in bed. The bed and the body were all full of blood. Apparently, she had managed to dial 9-1-1 on the phone after her husband headed downstairs. She never got to say much to the dispatcher before she was killed. But they had a lock on the address from the dispatcher. So at least the police knew where to go investigate."

"By the time the cops arrived, the intruder, or intruders were gone. They assumed that jewelry was stolen because there were two jewelry boxes broken open and emptied out. There was also a floor safe in the walk-in closet that was open, which they figured must have had some cash in it. All that was left in the safe were some legal papers."

"The Andersons were pretty well-off according to friends. George Anderson was a big-time stock broker for many years in Chicago. He had his own investment firm that was well known nationwide."

The chief then took me down to the kitchen. He said there was something very odd with the back door. We got to the kitchen, and he pointed to the back door. There was glass no glass on the kitchen floor. The door had six panels of glass with one broken out. The odd thing was that the glass was broken from the inside out. It was like someone was breaking out instead of in.

The bodies had been taken to Morry's Mortuary to have the local doctor do an autopsy. That's where I wanted to head next. I mentioned to Chief Turner that we should keep some of the facts out of the press. Such things as the open safe and broken glass in the door. We should also try to keep quiet that the electricity had been turned off. Some of it will probably leak out, but we needed to try and keep as much as possible quiet. It could be useful when questioning any suspects. I suggested we go to the mortuary next to see how the autopsy was coming along.

They were just finishing up with the autopsy on Mr. Anderson when we got there. The doctor was putting the organs back into the body cavity. The next step was stitching the chest back up. The chief introduced me to the doctor doing the autopsy. His name was Dr. Mark Adams.

I didn't enjoy watching bodies get cut up, but had seen enough of mangled bodies in the service and as a police officer. So, I knew what to expect going in, but I think it got to the chief because he had started to turn white and had to go outside right away. He claimed he had to make a phone call.

Things were pretty much as was figured. Both had multiple stab wounds, which was the cause of death. I wanted to see if we could figure out if the killer was right or left- handed and what type of knife was used. The doctor showed me the angle of the stab wounds and figured the killer was probably left-handed. We also figured the killer was about average height (around six foot), considering the downward angle on Mr. Andersons cuts.

The doctor also confirmed that they were probably killed between ten and twelve o'clock Saturday night. He got that from body temps, lividity, and the digestion of food in their stomachs. It coincided with the time of the 9-1-1 call from Anna. George was stabbed five times and Anna four times. It takes a heartless person to stab someone. Especially, to stab two people that viciously, just to rob them. It wasn't like they were going to get millions of dollars unless they happened to be in their will.

Well, I found out about all I could at the mortuary, and Dr. Adams had done a good job as far as I was concerned. He was pretty thorough for a country doc. The doc said he would send a copy of the autopsy and blood tests as soon as he got them written up. Next stop is the police station to get a copy of the police report and get a car to use.

Chapter 8

. . . .

I spent a couple of hours at the station going over the reports and talking to Rob Turner, the town's detective. He wasn't any too happy to be taking orders from me, but he answered my questions to the best of his knowledge. I told Rob, "I'm just here to help solve these murders as quickly as we can. I'm not here to take your job because I've had enough of police work to last me the rest of my life. Also, I'm not here to order you around, but would expect you to keep me informed of where you are going and anything you find out. The sooner we solve this the sooner I'll be out of your hair."

Rob said, "You'll have no problems with me. I admit I've had no experience in such matters, but have solved plenty of other cases."

I replied, "That's great, so let's get to work."

"Let's start with what we know. First the killer has to be a local person to know they had money and jewels. The killer was left-handed and probably around six foot tall. They also would have to either been a guest in the house or cased it out at some earlier time. I would think they probably were a guest at some time. If they cased it out, they would have done the robbery when no one was home. It didn't make sense to wait for the Andersons to be home and have to kill them."

"They didn't have much time between killing the Andersons and when the police arrived. They needed to be in and out quickly. They also need to know where the electric box was located and be able to get around the house in the dark. They would have to have gotten blood on themselves, because stabbing is very messy."

"There were some blood drops going up the stairs and a few near the bed. But all in all, there wasn't much spread around. And it seems the killer must not have gotten much on himself. He could have been wearing some protective outerwear possibly.

"There also should be a good chance somebody would have seen them because the house was in a residential neighborhood. Even though it was late in the evening, there's usually people up, being as it was Saturday. What really shocked me was that the glass was broken from the inside out. This bit of information we need to keep to ourselves for now. Especially since I had the same thing happen at my house."

"You had someone break the glass in the door at your house? Did you report it?"

"No, I wasn't sure if it was just some kids messing around or someone playing a prank on me. But it was kind of weird that my electricity was also turned off. But nothing was missing in the house that I could see."

"The list of things we don't know is a much larger list. We don't know if it was just one person, what the actual weapon was, or how they got into the house. It's hard to believe just one person could get in the house, cut off the electricity, kill two people, get the safe open and clean it and the jewelry boxes out. All of this before the cops showed up."

Rob then tells me, "I found out the cops didn't show up right away. There were two on duty. One was in Chaney having stopped at his house for a break with a friend. I'll let you guess what he was doing there. So, it took him awhile to get dressed and across town to the murder scene."

"The other officer was at Willow Lake taking care of a call of a house break-in. He caught the two intruders who happened to be two teenage kids. So the killer got a lucky break there. But he wouldn't have known about where the police were at the time."

Rob added, "It might not be related, but the next-door neighbor's dog was found dead the same night. When the police arrived next door, the Jensen's wondered why their dog wasn't barking. The dog had its own pen outside and it never made a sound. When they went out to see what the problem could be, they found him just lying there."

I told Rob to see if the dog's body was still available. If so, we needed to see how it died. Was it stabbed or possibly poisoned? I said, "We should start by splitting up and interviewing the neighbors and friends." I was hoping one of the neighbors might have seen someone coming and going or hanging around. Also, hopefully we could get some names of the Anderson's friends and relatives. I also had some figuring to do myself on how the glass had gotten broken on two doors at separate houses on the same night. And what was weirder was why they were broken from the inside out.

Rob and I spent the rest of Sunday talking to all the neighbors of the Andersons. No one had seen anything of value that night or the week leading up to it. We did manage to get a few names of friends of the Andersons. We decided to call it a day, and on Monday we'd start to track down any friends we could find.

I stopped at the diner for a late supper. Word was already all around town about me leading the investigation. So when I went in the diner for a bite to eat. The few people in there started asking a million questions. I, of course, had no answers for them. I didn't blame then for being worried. Someone just getting killed in a small town gets everyone upset. All I could do was tell everyone to keep their doors and windows locked and watch out for strangers.

Chapter 9

. . . .

June 10 Monday Morning

When Monday rolled around, I went to the diner early for breakfast. I got the same reception as the night before. At least there were no more reports of any killings. Not that I expected any. I thought I might have to start eating at home more if I wanted any privacy. So, I ordered my usual bacon, eggs, and hash browns. I try to keep my eating simple; it saves on your order getting screwed up. Plus, the waitress just has to say, the usual and I only have to say yes. I don't like to have a lot of conversation in the morning. I enjoy the peace and quiet of the morning.

I got to the station about eight o'clock, and we checked the fingerprints Rob had lifted from the Anderson house. They all seemed to match the Andersons, and there were no strange prints to be found. I figured the killer would have worn gloves. He probably wore something he could just throw away, as he had to get covered in blood.

Rob and I spent the day calling people and going out to interview the few people the Andersons spent time with. We had no luck on finding anything out of the ordinary. So the rest of the week was spent double-checking this and that, not really getting answers to anything. I was stumped, because there wasn't much to work with.

Rob did find out that the dog's body had been taken to the vet's office the next day. The Jensen's wanted to know what had caused their dog to die. He checked with the vet, and there were no outward signs of cause of death. We had to wait for the blood test results. They should have the results hopefully by tomorrow.

Chapter 10

. . . .

June 14 Friday Morning

Come Friday I decided to go fishing. I find I do my best thinking when fishing. I've always kind of figured that to catch fish you had to be in a good state of mind. Whenever I'm in a bad mood or feeling out of sorts I have never caught a damn thing. But if I'm feeling good and everything in the world seems to be in order, I have my best luck catching fish.

I headed out to Crabs Lake over by Chaney to fish. I have a favorite spot where I've had pretty good luck. It's a secluded area that's comprised of a small bay that's pretty well hidden from the rest of the lake. My idea of fishing is a comfortable place to sit and throw out a worm with a bobber. Then just sit back and relax and hope the bobber doesn't go under too often. It also doesn't hurt to have some beer on ice and cold fried chicken to help pass the time.

Today I figured I was on the job, so I skipped the beer and chicken. I needed to relax and think about this murder case. One problem is that if you get too comfortable, it's very easy to fall asleep. So not only did I not catch any fish but didn't come up with any ideas about the case. But I did catch a brief nap.

I decided it had to probably be someone that lived in the area, and probably worked here too. Someone working out of town wouldn't really have the time or knowledge to check out facts. Such as the Andersons daily routines and their finances. That's not something a stranger would know. Plus, they would have a tough time finding it out. We also found out that the neighbor dog had been killed with rat poison. So, the murder suspect had to know about the dog ahead of time.

My next move was going to be spending Friday and Saturday nights at the local bars. Alcohol has a way of loosening lips. I figured I'd split this job with Rob. I gave him a call and explained my thinking. He thought it was about the only thing left to do at this point.

I've lived a lot of my life here in Black Crow. I was born in Black River Falls, Wisconsin in 1955. We moved to Black Crow in 1965 when I was ten years old. And I lived here until the start of my junior year in high school. We then moved to Missouri where my dad got a job with the conservation department there. When I finished high school, I went into the service. That makes me thirty-eight years old now. I'm about six foot two and weigh in at around two hundred twenty pounds. I've always been in good shape and don't believe in working out. I always figured that our bodies are like a car. There're only so many miles you can go before you start breaking down. So, I figure why push it.

Both of my parents are deceased from cancer. I figure my chances of dying the same way are pretty good, so I try to live life to the fullest. That's why I quit the police force and bummed around for a couple of years. After four years in the Army, I put three years in the Wisconsin State Patrol. I got sick of taking care of traffic accidents on the interstate highway. So, I got hired by the Madison Police Department. I spent ten years there first doing routine patrol work and the last five years as a detective. In my spare time I worked in construction with a friend remodeling houses around the Madison area.

So, after a couple of years I came back to Black Crow. I rented a house for a while and did small repair and remodeling around the area. Finally, I bought my house and started remodeling it. I've never been married and have no kid's, that I know of, so I'm kind of a free bird. I'm still looking for that perfect woman. Maybe my standards are too high. But I am working on this as we speak.

It's Friday evening, about eight o'clock, so I get ready to head out to hang at the local bars and see what I can hear. We have quite a few bars in the area. With three towns and lakes, we get a lot of out-of-towners on the weekends. Most locals seem to frequent the town bars. I started with the Black Crow and Heron Lake area. Rob took the other two towns and lakes as they're smaller and there are fewer bars. We have four bars in Black Crow, and two on Lake Heron. I spent about an hour and a half in each and didn't hear anything worthwhile. There was some talk of the killings, but just what was read in the newspapers.

Chapter 11

. . . .

June 15 Saturday Morning

Saturday I checked in with Rob, and he had the same results. So, we decided to swap bars on Saturday night so we didn't seem so conspicuous. Well, Saturday night had the same results. I don't know what's worse—doing stakeouts or sitting in bars trying not to drink too much. Technically were on duty, but it's not like were on the big city police force and have strict rules. I'm not worried about getting fired, but I have a tendency of not backing down from anything, especially when drinking. This can lead to fights and having the police called. I really don't need that since I'm supposed to be on the police force now. Don't get me wrong, I've always claimed to be a lover not a fighter. But, there's nothing like a good fight to get the blood flowing. Of course, lovemaking can do the same thing. I guess that's why I enjoy both.

Anyways I decide to call it a night at around one o'clock and head home. I pull into my driveway and head for the back door. That's when I notice the house is dark and the yard light is off. My first thought is that this can't be happening again. I grab the flashlight out of the truck and head for the door.

I probably should be carrying a gun, but didn't want to get back into that again. But I might have to rethink that idea. I grab a piece of scrap wood from the pile I have by the back door, figuring that's better than nothing. I go in the porch and as I step to the kitchen door, I hear glass crunch under my feet. I shine the light down and I'll be damned if it isn't glass from the door. The same pane is broken out of the door that I just fixed a week ago. I really hate fixing things twice. Now I'm more pissed off and perplexed than afraid. What's really dumb is that the door is still locked. I reach in and unlock the dead bolt, then open the door. I go through the same routine I did a week ago.

I go to the basement to turn on the electricity and then check out the house. Everything is in order and I find nothing missing. I figure I'd better call this in, just to have a record. I call in and talk to Jim, the night dispatcher. He sends a squad car out to the house to have it written up. After we get that written up and I convince the officer that he doesn't have to check the house out, I decide to get some sleep.

Chapter 12

. . . .

June 16 early Sunday Morning

I crawl into bed at about three o'clock and just about fall asleep when the phone rings. It's Rob and he says we might have another murder. He just got a call from the dispatcher saying there is something going on over in Chaney. The caller said something funny is going on next door to him. An officer went there to check it out, and it looked like it was a break-in.

I got the address and threw my clothes on and headed out. Rob beat me there and was waiting to go in with me. Rob's nephew, the chief's son Tim was the officer that took the call and checked out the house. He said he found the back-door glass broken out and the door unlocked. He went in and found a man's body all bloody lying at the foot of the upstairs doorway. He then said he rushed outside because it made him sick. He then called it in.

We went around to the back door. The back door was unlocked and the glass had been broken from the inside out. I had remembered to grab my pistol on the way out of my house. I still had my Glock pistol, which I bought while working on the Madison PD. I figured I'd better start carrying it seeing as I'm back working again.

I told Rob to wait a minute. I ran to my car and grabbed some shoe protectors and latex gloves for us to use. I gave Rob a set and then put mine on. I told Rob it would help preserve the scene.

We entered the house with guns and flashlights drawn. The electricity was apparently off, which was no surprise. We found nothing in the kitchen, but there was that old familiar coppery smell in the air. That's never a good sign because I knew it meant blood.

We found the elderly man at the foot of the stairs leading to the second floor. There was blood all over the front of him. He had a pistol in his hand, but I had a feeling that he never got a shot off. We checked him for a pulse, but found none. So, we stepped around the blood to go up the stairs. There were bloody footprints in the carpet going upstairs. But they had no pattern to them, so the killer must have worn shoe covers just like we had on.

We checked the rooms upstairs and found nothing until we got to the back bedroom. It was apparently the master bedroom. In there we found an elderly woman on the bed with her chest and abdomen full of blood. In checking her vitals, we found her to be gone too. This did not look like a killing of passion as all the wounds were in the chest area. If they were crimes of passion, there are usually cut wounds all over the body. She appeared to have died instantly as I didn't see any defensive marks on her.

I told Rob to call the state police to have their techs go over the place. We took a look around and noticed all dresser and chest drawers were ransacked. In their walk-in closet there was a safe built into the floor. Its door was open and there was nothing but some papers inside. This makes two safes that had been found open at two different murders. It almost had to be someone that could crack a safe without blowing it open or they somehow knew the combinations.

As we checked the rest of the house, we also found another strange thing. When we went to the basement to turn the power back on, we found a freezer. It was at the opposite end of the basement from the power box. It was a chest type freezer and the top was open. We went over and found wrapped meat and other various frozen foods strewn all over the floor. The freezer itself was just about empty. I've seen some strange things in my time, but these murders had some new twists.

I told officer Tim, that had been called to check out the break-in, to secure the area and put up crime scene tape. I asked if he touched anything in the house when he first got there. He said that when he entered and saw a man's body on the floor, he checked to see if he was alive. He then exited the house and called it in.

We headed outside to interview the neighbors, hoping someone saw something. Problem is that a lot of these neighborhoods have elderly, retired people and they usually go to bed fairly early.

The first people we talked to were the Martez's from next door. They were the people that called in that something strange was going on next door. The deceased couple's names were Ed and Carol Browning. They had moved up here from Glendale, Illinois about eight years ago. Ed was retired from insurance sales for about ten years now.

The Martez's said it was a little after eleven o'clock went they pulled into their driveway. They had been on a trip out of town and were just getting back. As they were walking to their house from the car all the yard and security lights next door went out. They hauled their suitcases into their house and went to look out the window to check out next door. At first they didn't see anything. They figured that maybe it was a case of their main fuse or breaker going off.

They went and emptied their suitcases and got everything put away. About half an hour later they went and looked at the Browning's house next door and saw it was still dark. They tried calling the Browning's with no luck. Then Fred Mertz said he went next door and rang the doorbell. It didn't seem to be working, so he banged on the door. When he got no answer, he went back to his house. That's when he decided to call the police.

They could see somewhat next door from their own outside lights. They thought they might have seen a figure run into the woods behind the Browning house after the Browning's lights went out. But they couldn't be sure because it was still too dark.

I asked if they knew anything about the Browning financial status. They only knew that Ed didn't trust banks. He remembered the great depression and how everyone lost their life savings. He had been very adamant about not using any banks. Word was that Ed and Carol had paid cash for their house. One would think he probably had a lot of cash hidden somewhere. I figured we could learn more if we could find some relatives.

There were some pictures in the living room of what looked like two young families. The Martez's said that Ed and Carol had a daughter and son, both with families of their own. They didn't know how to get ahold of them, though. So, we looked on the backs of the pictures and found the families' names. We also checked in the cell phones we found and got the phone numbers for the son and daughter.

I thought we'd better do the death notification right now instead of waiting until morning. So, I first called the son, John, and informed him of his parent's deaths. He was, of course, pretty upset and said he had just talked to them earlier from the hospital. They had just gone to bed, but were going to get backup and come up to the hospital. John said he called at about ten fifteen. I informed him that it was a break-in and robbery. When he asked how they died, I said it was a stabbing, but it was quick so they didn't suffer.

He said he couldn't come down until probably Sunday night or Monday. He explained that his wife was in the hospital and had emergency surgery about three hours ago. He was waiting for her to come out of ICU. She had a stroke and they had to go in and clear the artery. It was still touch and go with her condition.

The neighbors had taken their two children, but they had to go to work on Monday morning. So, he was in a tight spot on when he could get up here. They live in Green Bay, so it's not too far away. He asked for my phone number and said he'd get back to me as soon as he knew what was happening.

I told him how sorry I was about his parents and his wife. I hoped she would make a full recovery. I asked if he minded answering a couple of quick questions for me. He said that's no problem as he was just sitting and waiting for his wife to wake up.

My first question was if he knew how much money his parents might have kept in the house. He didn't know, but thought it was probably quite a bit. He said his dad didn't believe in banks. But he wouldn't have any idea how much money there might be or where it might be.

Next, I asked if he would have any idea why the intruders would have emptied the freezer out. John said he wasn't sure, but there was probably money hidden in there. It was common knowledge among elderly folks that it was reasonably safe to hide money in a freezer. And he said his dad used to always joke about keeping cold hard cash at his disposal.

Lastly, I asked if his parents had been worried about anything or anyone lately. Also, if they had seemed to act any different, anything out of the ordinary. John said everything seemed normal, and they had just been up to visit a couple of weeks earlier. I asked if he wanted me to call his sister or if he preferred to. He said he would call her and give her the news. She was in Florida with her family on vacation. Her name is Diane Ames. I thanked him and wished his wife well and said I would see him when he made it down here.

So, Rob and I walked around to the back of the house looking for any possible tracks that might have been left by the suspect. We checked all the way to the woods and saw nothing. We decided to come back in the daylight to do a better search. So, next up was to interview all the neighbors. We had to hope the Madison crime analysts could find something. It was still nagging me that the safes were open at both crime scenes. You had to be pretty skilled to open a safe. The suspects also didn't have much time to open them. I told Rob our next step was to try and find if there were any ex-convicted thieves living in the area.

This had to be someone that lived in the area. Being this was June, there were probably around three thousand people between the towns and the lakes. My feeling was to lean towards the local folks. You would have to have lived around here awhile to know who has money and who doesn't. People probably know that I have money, but it's all invested or in the bank.

The other problem I have is why my house got broken into the same nights the murders occurred. And my break-ins seemed to be after the murders. But I had nothing taken that I could find. I asked Rob if he could make a list of probable people to check out. And if he would also check local records for any possible break-ins in the past.

I headed home to try and get a few hours of sleep. I also wanted to double-check my house again for any other clues that might be there. There was nothing amiss in my place, and I figured to fix my broken door pane in the morning. I hit the sack and set the alarm for ten o'clock in the morning.

Chapter 13

. . . .

June 12 Sunday Midmorning

The alarm woke me at ten o'clock, so I got up and hit the shower to clear my head. I thought some coffee and breakfast would be good before fixing the door pane. So, of course, I went down to Barb's diner. It's open seven days a week for breakfast. It's a pretty busy place on Sunday because of the church-goers. I'm not a big one for attending church. I do believe in God and think religion is good. But I believe in doing my praying in private.

Anyways I ordered my usual bacon, eggs, and hash browns with plenty of coffee. I do love my cholesterol, but I add some orange juice or tomato juice to balance things out. While I'm waiting, our beloved mayor, John Jones, or JJ for short, sits down next to me. I figure that's all I need is him nagging me about the murders. Especially on Sunday morning.

JJ asks, "How you doing today, Duke? Kind of late for breakfast, isn't it? Must have been out and about last night."

I answer, "I'm doing about as well as can be expected. And I was actually working last night."

He starts telling me that a lot of the local folks are starting to get worried. I tell him that I don't blame them. He asks if we have any leads at all. There is not much I can tell him. So, I tell him we haven't found much in the way of evidence or clues to either crime. And I inform him that I have the state police working the latest crime scene. He said, "Do you think that's wise; it will make us look like bumbling fools."

I replied, "They have more people and equipment to analyze the scene and a great lab at their disposal. We need to find some clues if we want to have any chance of solving these murders." JJ finally agreed that was probably the best way to go. Thankfully he then got up and left.

John isn't a bad guy, but his attitude can be irritating. He has lived in Black Crow all of his life. His family had been some of the founders of our town back in the early years. He was a couple of years ahead of me in school, so I hadn't had much to do with him. He seemed to be an all right guy from what I knew and heard.

As I was finishing my breakfast, a guy in a suit came up to me and asked if I was Duke Moran. I said I was and he asked if he could sit and talk to me. I agreed, and he sat and introduced himself. He told me he was Joe Blaine, a special investigator from the state. He flashed his badge and ID at me. He was one of the special investigators from the Madison police. He said he had heard good things about me from some of the guys on the force. I still had a few friends left down there I talked to once in a while.

He said he dropped a copy of their report at the police station, but wanted to go over it with me in person. They told him at the station that I might be here for breakfast.

There were no surprises. They found no strange fingerprints or any trace evidence anywhere. I asked about footprints going into the woods. Joe said it has been so dry from the lack of rain that the ground was too hard to leave any prints. They figured the perp wore gloves, but would have probably gotten blood on himself or themselves if it was more than one person. It's pretty hard to stab someone multiple times without blood flying all over the place.

There were some small specks of blood on the glass broken out of the door. That was probably because they used the killing knife to break out the glass when leaving. We'll know better once we analyze the blood. There also was no sign of a break-in. The lock was probably picked to gain entrance. Joe said he was heading back to Madison and if he thought of anything else, he would call. He also gave me his phone number to call if I needed anything. We said goodbye to each other as I paid my bill.

I decided to run over to the crime scene to have another look around. Being it was Sunday morning, it was pretty quiet around town. Rob had left me a message that he was going to church at nine o'clock. He would find out where I was after church. Probably around ten fifteen depending on how long-winded the parson is today.

I got to the house and did a walk around the outside. It's a two-story house and not that much different from the Anderson house. It wasn't all remodeled, though, like the Anderson house. But it was still a nice house. I noticed it had all the original woodwork in it yet. I checked windows and doors for signs of illegal entry. Just as Joe Blaine had said, there was no sign of any scratches or abrasions anywhere. For an old house it was in excellent shape.

I took a walk back to the woods and walked into it. It's only about one hundred yards deep, but pretty thick except for the trails. On the backside there's another street with only two houses on it. One house is empty and for sale. I walked over to it and took a look around. There is no sign of any activity around the grounds. I look into what windows I can. But the house is empty of any furniture and is locked up tight as a drum.

I walk down to the other house and knock on the door. A younger woman answers the door and I tell her who I am. She asks for identification and I show her my old badge and ID from when I was a Madison detective. She doesn't look too close to question the police department it's from. She invites me into the house and asks if I'd like anything to drink. I decline and say I just have a few questions for her.

I ask if she was home on Saturday night when the break-in occurred. She said she was and I asked if she saw anyone around or any strange vehicles in the area Saturday. She said there was a white van parked up by the corner at around eleven o'clock. She saw it when she was locking up the house before going to bed.

It didn't bother her because people park around there quite frequently. She said they usually combine in one vehicle to go out or do whatever their evening plans are. They were usually picked up after bar time or the next morning. She thought she heard an engine start up just as she was falling asleep. That would have been probably between eleven fifteen and eleven thirty.

She said she lives alone with her daughter. The daughter had been asleep since about ten o'clock. So, I'm thinking we might have our first clue. I thank her after she lets me know that she couldn't tell what kind of van it was. She also couldn't tell if there was anything on the sides, such as writing or logos. It was too far away and too dark.

So I decide to go back to my house. Most people that went to church are getting home now. I decide to question my neighbors about my break-in. There are only five other houses on my street. All of our lots are about two acres each, so were pretty well spread out from each other. I also have woods behind my house and on the west side. If you go through the woods in the back, you'll come out on Heron Lake.

I start with the neighbors on the east of me. Jack and Jenny Houser are home and their two kids are outside playing. I get together once in a while with them for cookouts. I see Jack sitting in a lawn chair watching the kids play while drinking a beer. He offers me one as I walk up to their house. I decline, saying maybe later. I plan to mow my yard, which will work up a good thirst, as the temperature is on the rise. It's supposed to get close to eighty degrees today.

I ask Jack if he's seen anything of people or vehicles that seem out of the ordinary in the neighborhood. He says he hasn't noticed anything or anybody unusual. He hollers to Jenny to come outside where we are. I ask her the same questions I asked Jack. She says she hasn't noticed anything either.

I also mention a white van. Jenny says it seems that she might have noticed a white van go through the neighborhood a couple of times during the day. She wasn't sure as she was cleaning and just caught a glance out of the corner of her eye. She just assumed it was a service vehicle from some business.

They asked why I was asking the questions. I just told them I thought someone might have tried to get in my garage. I have a lot of tools in there and didn't want to lose any of them. They said they would keep an eye out for anything strange. I thank them and head to the other neighbors.

I went to the other four houses on our street and talked to all of them. Nobody had noticed anything unusual. In fact, most say it's been a pretty quiet summer, except for the kids. They had all heard that I was investigating the murder and were worried about their safety. I just reminded them to keep their homes locked and be wary of any strangers. And I asked if they did see anything out of place to let me know.

My best guess about the break-ins of my house are someone coming from the woods. I decide to take a walk back to the lake and check it out. When I get to the water, I check around the small clearing there. There's a path wide enough for vehicles to come back there. And there are several tire tracks in the clearing. If you park there you wouldn't be seen by any houses. It's part of the lake where no one lives. The nearest road is about a half a mile away. It's probably a great spot for young couples to park and make out. I don't see anything else to look for back here so I head back to my house.

You probably wonder why I don't fish back here instead of going over to Crabs Lake. For one thing I tried back here but never even got a nibble. I know there's fish in the lake, but they must be in other parts of the lake. I have thought about seeing if I can build a dock back here. Then I could keep a boat handy. But I wouldn't be able to watch it. And I could just see some kids sneak back here and take it out on the water. I'm sure I'd be liable if anything happened to them. So, I guess that won't happen. I head back to my place.

Well, it's time to mow the lawn. I let it go too long, so I've got my work cut out for me now. It's a beautiful day with temperatures in the upper seventies so far. So, I trim first with my walk-behind mower, then get the rider out to do the rest. Two acres can be quite a bit to mow.

I've got a spot in my yard that has been bugging me. You ever have a spot in your yard where the grass just doesn't want to grow decent? Usually it's under a tree. My bad spot is next to the house on the east side. The weird thing is that it's square. It's about ten feet by ten feet, against the house. My guess is that there was once a room on that end of the house. There is no evidence of a door inside the house. Unless that's what the window there used to be. I've tried reseeding it and giving it extra water. But it just stays the same. Oh well, I better get the mowing done so then I can enjoy a couple of beers.

After mowing I was sitting next door at Jack's house having a beer when I see a car pull into my driveway. I recognize the beautiful lady getting out of the car. Her name is Jane Downing, and I guess you could call her my girlfriend.

We have a kind of loose relationship. We enjoy the company of each other, but don't know about living together. We are pretty set in our ways, and so far the relationship has worked just fine. We do our own thing, but spend a fair amount of time together.

I shout at her to see if she wants to come over for a cold one. Instead she waves me to come over there. So, I thank Jack for the beer, and tell him "Things look much better over at my place. No offense meant." He agrees with me and says, "No offense taken, and have fun."

Jane is thirty-four years old and looks to be about twenty. She's just one very beautiful lady. I call her Jane Doe because of her big gorgeous brown eyes. They just melt you down. I admit that I'm helpless when she looks at me. I would lay my life down for this lady, that's how much I think of her.

I walk towards her, trying not to run and look too eager. I haven't seen her for about two weeks, and that animal in my shorts in going crazy. We embrace and kiss, or should I say we try to devour each other. Apparently, she has missed me too. She purrs in my ear and says I'd better get her to my bed before she attacks me out here in the yard. She doesn't have to tell me twice.

I manage to get her in the door where we start kissing again and groping to get our clothes pulled off. We manage to get up the stairs, leaving a trail of clothes along the way. Jane didn't have a whole lot of clothes on to start with. Just sandals, shorts, and a tee shirt. No bra or panties, which I find very erotic.

I can't put into words what this lady looks like. She could be a *Playboy* centerfold easily. Her breasts are perfect. Not small, but at the same time not huge. I've always said what doesn't fit in your mouth just goes to waste anyways. And there's plenty to go to waste with Jane. She also has very dark brown hair to go with the dark brown eyes. I don't know what this gorgeous lady sees in me, but I'm not questioning her. I'm just going to enjoy, enjoy, enjoy.

Anyways we get to the bedroom and kind of skip most of the foreplay. Were both on fire and need to get right down to business. I guess I'm too slow for her because she pushes me onto the bed and jumps on top of me. I don't mind being on the bottom. Actually, I rather enjoy it. Looking up at this beautiful creature and watching her work herself into a climax. When she does come, it reminds me of a radio station that has women call in and give their best vocal climax. Jane would have won, hands down. Just the sound of her got me so aroused that I couldn't hold back anymore. If I would have died right then and there, I would have been a very happy man.

After we spent some time kissing, we swapped positions. Then we made out and made love very slowly. But that didn't stay slow very long. We had worked ourselves up again and ended up climaxing together in the arms of each other. After we cooled down some, Jane said she was ready for that beer now. I went down for a couple of beers while Jane got the shower going. I got back upstairs, and we enjoyed a beer and shower together. Just living the life.

Jane left at about eleven o'clock to go to her place for some sleep. Jane said if she didn't go home there wouldn't be much sleeping done. She has to get up early for a long day at work. Jane owns a small floral shop and has just one employee. So, when floral sales are up from weddings and such, she is pretty busy. So, this means I get some badly needed sleep too.

Chapter 14

. . . .

June 17 Monday Morning

Monday morning I'm up at seven o'clock and jump in the shower. I'm in the middle of shaving after my shower when my cell phone rings. I look at the caller ID and see it's a call from out of our area. Chances are good it's some telemarketer. I figure I had better answer it with all that's going on. It's Ed and Carol Browning's son John calling.

He asks if we've caught the person or persons that killed his mother and father. I reluctantly told him we haven't figured out who did it yet. I said we've got a couple of clues and we're still working hard at it. He informs me his wife is doing fine and already up and walking.

John said he would be up today as soon as he could get the kids to school and set up someone to pick them up from school. I told him to call me when he gets to town, and I'd talk to him then.

I decided to make a stop at Barb's Diner for a quick coffee and maybe a roll. I get to Barb's and find my favorite seat as Barb walks up to wait on me. She says that the word is out about the killing Saturday night. She felt really bad because Ed came in every morning for coffee during the week. I was kind of surprised because I hadn't ever noticed him. Barb said he came in at ten o'clock with four other retired guys. I never came in that late, so that's probably why I never saw him. I asked her who he met every morning. I got my notebook out so I could get the names.

She said their names were Ernie Clark, George Fennimore, Charley Jones and Jim Knowles. I asked if Charley Jones was related to our beloved major.

Barb said he was a cousin to JJ's father. I decided it might be a good idea to come in and talk to the four men and get more of a line on Ed Browning's life.

I head to the station to meet with Rob and see if he came up with anything new. Once there the dispatcher tells me the chief wants a meeting to see what progress we've made. I went to the conference room to see if they had a whiteboard we could use. I didn't see one in there, and Rob happened to walk in. I asked him about a whiteboard, and he thought there might be one in the storeroom out in the rear of the building. So, he went to look for it, and I went to the coffee maker for another cup of coffee.

The chief walked in at the same time Rob showed up rolling a big whiteboard into the conference room. I told the chief that we need to make a list of what we knew and what we needed to check out yet. I told Rob he could do the writing as we wouldn't be able to read it if I wrote it.

I told him to label the first column with what we know. Then label the next column Things to check on.

What We Know	Need to Check
Killer probably left-handed	Interview Browning's son John
Probably only one suspect	Interview daughter Diane Ames
Killer probably about 6 ft. tall	Interview 4 men in coffee clutch
Might drive white van	check out van owners in area
Probably local person	re-interview neighbors
Friendly with victims	get list of stolen jewelry
Can pick locks and safes?	check pawnshops in Madison
who installed floor safes	

The chief asked how sure we are on the things we think we know. So, I explained that the killer was probably left-handed because of the angle of the stab wounds. The angle also tells us that the killer was about average height. Somewhere around six feet tall. Chances are it was a man. It had to be someone strong enough to overpower the victims. There is the slight chance it could be a woman. But I didn't feel that it was a woman. Women seem to have more tender feelings towards most people unless it was someone that hurt them badly. Such as a cheating spouse. You see them hugging other people more often and show more emotion than men usually do.

As for the white van, there had been sightings of one in the area at various times. They were very brief sightings and there are probably quite a few white vans in our area.

The suspect almost has to be a local person. They need time to scope out the victim's houses and routines. A stranger would have stood out and been noticed by someone. He also knew about the dog next door to the Anderson's house.

It's not a lot of facts, but it's more than we had a week ago. I said that I'd start with interviewing the son when he gets into town. I also was going to get together with the four men that Ed Browning had coffee with every day. That was going to be at ten o'clock this morning. I would also talk to Ed and Carol Browning's daughter. She is on vacation in Florida, and I don't know when she would be coming yet.

I asked Rob to see about a list of jewelry. I said he could check with the insurance companies the victims had. They usually have a list and sometimes pictures of any insured jewelry. If we find that, then we could start checking out pawnshops within a hundred-mile radius. It's a long shot, but we could get lucky.

I also asked Rob to get on the computer and see if he could get a list of white vans in our area. I'm computer illiterate, but I know it can save a lot of time and effort to check things out. A list of white vans would help a lot. It was also a long shot, but we would take anything we could find to get more leads.

Later on in the day, we could start re-interviewing the neighbors at both locations. People have had time to think and maybe something would be remembered. So, we had plenty to work on and would be busy for at least the next couple of days.

I went to the diner at about nine forty-five to talk with the coffee clutch. I had a seat at the counter and Barb brought me a cup of coffee. She said it was unusual to see me in here at this hour. I told her I was here to talk to the four guys that Ed Browning met with. At ten o'clock four men walked in together. Barb told me they were the men I was waiting for. I asked her which one was related to our beloved Mayor. She pointed him out and I thanked her.

I walked over to the four men as soon as they seemed to be settled and had put their orders in. I introduced myself by name and told them I was helping the police department to solve to two murders. Of course, their first question to me were the two murders, or actually four people murdered, tied together. I replied that they probably were. Without going into detail, I said there were similarities in both.

They all introduced themselves to me and that they really felt bad about Ed and his wife. Ed had joined their group about a year ago. Charley Jones said he met Ed at a VFW get-together. Both men were veterans from the Army and both served in Germany during the war. I asked how the rest of them of them happened to get together. It happens the four of them play golf three days a week, in the afternoon. They said that Ed would fill in when one of the others couldn't make it.

We do have a golf course here in Black Crow. It's actually pretty swanky for being in the north woods and such a small town. But as I said before, we get a lot of Illinois people up here. The course's name is The Whispering Pines. Its twenty-seven holes total.

The main eighteen holes were designed by a pro golfer that passed away years ago. It can be very challenging to the novice player. The other nine holes are all par three holes. But it's a very, very challenging nine holes. It's a lot of fun, but can ruin your day. There's big oak tree in front of five of the holes. One hole had water around three quarters of it. The other three are severe doglegs with a lot of water. I manage to get out once in a while at the course, but I prefer fishing. It's easier on the nerves.

It's considered a country club, but is open to the public. Membership runs a thousand dollars a year for unlimited golf with riding cart. Plus, you have to spend at least a hundred dollars a month in the clubhouse for either food or golf accessories.

I asked if anyone could fill me in a little on Ed's life to give me an idea what kind of guy he was. They all agree that he was a great guy and was devoted to his wife, Carol. She was his second wife and they had a son and daughter together. My next question to them was if Ed had been acting any different lately or complained about anything. They all agreed that he was acting pretty much normal. They said he always complained about the prices of everything always going up. He wouldn't buy the golf membership because he figured he might save a few bucks by paying each time he went.

I then asked if they ever heard Ed talk about money and banks. This question got them all going and all talking at once. I settled them down and asked to hear from one at a time. Ernie Clark spoke up first. He was a short stocky man, looking to be in his sixties. He said Ed was dead set against banks. He remembered the great depression and how his parents lost everything. Apparently, they owned two farms and were looking to buy a third when the great depression hit. The banks ended up taking everything including the money they had in bank.

George Fennimore spoke next. He looked to be way over six feet tall and bald as a bowling ball. He added that Ed had told them once about a trick the German immigrants used to hide their money years ago. These were the German immigrants that had gone into farming. They usually had grain bins for oats and silos for silage. When they would fill these from the harvest, they used them as their banks.

They would put money in several canning jars. Then as they filled the grain and silos, they would put a jar of money in every so often. That way it got covered up in several layers. Then through the next year as they fed the cattle the grain and corn, a jar would appear every so often. This usually worked out so they had money when the last batch was getting low. It was almost like getting a regular paycheck. And it was a pretty safe way to protect your money.

So Ed said he used that same principle. He never said how he did it, but mentioned that he always had cold cash on hand. My first thought was the emptied-out freezer. I made sure not to mention this as it was a fact we were keeping to ourselves.

Now I'm thinking it had to be someone that knew the Browning's. The killer wouldn't have had enough time to search the whole house. I'm sure that Ed probably told other people about his cold cash. So, it had to be someone that was friendly with the Browning's.

Jim Knowles spoke up saying that Ed was either well-to-do or poor. He said he was so tight with money that he squeaked when he walked. Ed was always looking for deals on golf, and complaining it cost too much. He also used coupons when going out to eat and saving some of the food to take home. That way he said he got two meals for the price of one.

It was hard to even get him to buy a round of drinks when golfing. But the general consensus was that he probably had plenty of money.

I didn't get much more out of the four men, so I told them to let me know if they thought of anything else. It was close to lunchtime, so I went to my favorite booth to have lunch.

I got my order in to Barb and figured I had some time to sort things out and figure my next move.

Next thing I know, in walks our wonderful mayor. I thought that if I was going to keep running into him here, maybe I'd start eating somewhere else.

JJ stopped to talk to his dad's cousin and the others at that table. After about ten minutes, he saw me and headed over. He took a seat without being invited and said hello. He made some small talk at first. Eventually he got around to the investigation. I informed him that we were working on it full time and had a couple of leads. I said that I couldn't go into what we had. He wasn't too happy about that but eventually got up and left.

I got to the station at around one o'clock. Rob was there, and we got down to exchanging what we found out.

Rob had made a list of the white vans in and around our three towns and lakes. He said there was the possibility that some of the out-of-towners might have some. But I told him it was probably a local person. The reason being that the freezer at the Browning's probably had money in it. It would have to be someone they knew that somehow heard Ed say he had cold cash. I laid out the story he told about the German farmers. Rob agreed so we decided to go over his list of vans.

The names were mostly people I didn't know. Most were for businesses in the area. I know my buddy Eddy had one for his job. The only other name I recognized was John Jones, the mayor. John and Eddy are not related as far as I know.

John has a rodent control business. So it could have been his truck people saw because he drives all over for his business. He also has immediate access to rat poison. But then so does everyone in the area. You can buy it at the hardware store, plus even the grocery stores sell it. Some of the gas stations that carry snack items also carry it.

There were ten names on the list Rob had come up with. I told Rob to check their names out in the computer first to see if any had records or anything else that would pop up.

The computer was in its early years, but Madison law enforcement had been feeding a lot of info into the system the last couple of years. After that I said we would go around and see if the vans were still used and talk to the owners.

Rob goes off to get on the computer and I head for the coffee pot. On my way there, I notice a man walk in the front of the office. The clerk calls out to me while I'm pouring coffee. I have a visitor asking to see me. It's Ed and Carol Browning's son, John. I wave him back and when he gets to me, I ask if he would like some coffee.

He says, "That would be great. I could use a little caffeine today." I get him a cup and take him to the interview room. I tell him how sorry I am about his parents. I add that I'd like to ask him some questions, and then we need him to make a positive ID of their bodies.

He agrees, so I start out getting some personal history on the family. He doesn't have anything much to add that I didn't already know. He didn't know of any people they spent time with around here. He told me he, his wife, and kids came here once or twice a summer for a couple of days. Mostly so the kids could enjoy the lake. His dad had a pontoon boat in a slip down at the marina. But usually Ed and Carol came up to visit them in Green Bay. They came up quite a bit in the winter because they had Packers season tickets.

"They had four tickets, so we got to go see a lot of football games because of it. But I need to add that my wife and I had to pay for our tickets. Dad said he could sell them for a lot of money, depending on how the season was going. That's how tight my dad was with money. Plus, we would put them up for usually two nights and that meant feeding them. I didn't mind because that's how I was brought up. But it really bugged my wife. Her family was the exact opposite. They'd give you the shirt off their back and not charge you for it."

John asked about getting his parents' bodies so they could plan their funeral. I told him as soon as the autopsies were done, which should be any time now.

I took John over to Morry's Mortuary to view the bodies. I called first to make sure they were ready. After we were through there, I said my goodbyes to John and went back to the police station to check on Rob.

Rob had just finished checking out the owners of the white vans when I got there. He said only one person had any record at all. They were two moving violations for speeding. His name was Joe Dumont and we decided to start with him. We figured we'd go now as it was only four o'clock.

Joe Dumont was at home luckily and invited us in after we knocked. He had a small house in the small town of Chaney. It was well cared for on the outside and the inside was neat and clean. He had a wife and two children. He seemed to be a decent clean-cut guy. We told Joe and his wife that we were checking out people in the three lakes area that owned white vans.

I asked Joe where he was on Saturday night the sixteenth. Joe said they had a cookout with the neighbors. That lasted until about ten o'clock. Then they put the kids to bed and his wife and he watched and old movie on TV. They went to bed about one o'clock and that was it for the night. Joe's wife backed him up on that and gave us the neighbors name to check it out. I also asked if he was left or right-handed. He replied that he was right-handed. He was wearing a watch on his left, which is normal for a right-handed person.

We thanked them and made a quick stop at the neighbor's to confirm Joe's alibi. They told us pretty much the same story, so that seemed to clear that van. We decided to call it a day and continue in the morning.

Chapter 15

. . . .

June 18 Tuesday Morning

Tuesday morning I went to breakfast and then headed to the station. Rob was there, and the first thing I asked him was if he came up with any new ideas. He said he checked through the paperwork at both victims' homes for any insurance papers. He had calls into both to see if they listed the jewelry the ladies had. He hoped to hear something by the end of the day.

When checking for insurance policies, he found all the victims were covered. The Andersons had thirty thousand dollars on each of them. They had no kids, so the beneficiaries were a bunch of charities.

The Browning's had just ten thousand dollars on each other. It was left to their two children. Basically, it was just enough to bury them.

We decided to try and get the rest of the white vans checked out today. I said that I would vouch for Eddy Jones as I've known him for years. I also know he was out of town during the first break-in. So, we scratched him off the list.

We went to Jane's Flower Power Shop first. Jane was in and we told her about checking all white van owners in the area. We asked if she kept a log of her deliveries each day. She said they didn't but most of their deliveries were to the nearby hospital and to businesses all over the three towns.

I asked where the van is at night and if anyone uses it overnight. She said no one uses it after six o'clock and its kept locked in the backend of the shop. And she said no one had access to the key but her.

Next, we stopped at DJ Appliance Repair shop. And as luck would have it, Dave was working on a washing machine in the shop. The J in the name is for his wife Jane. We told Dave our reason for being there. We asked where he and his van were on the nights of the two murders. He said he takes his van home at night, but never works past six o'clock. He said he catches hell from his wife if he's late for supper. Dave is in his sixties, and although his alibi isn't real strong, he doesn't seem like he would be hard up enough to kill for money. I did note his watch was on his left wrist, which meant he was probably right-handed.

Our next one on the list we decide to check is John Jones, the mayor. We decide to call him first because his business is kind of part time. He also spends time at the municipal building doing whatever it is that a mayor does.

John happened to be at his house when we called. He runs his business out of his house and garage. We said we'd be over in about ten minutes to ask some questions. He said he'd be glad to help in any way that he could.

Once we got to his house, he invited us into his office. It was a spare bedroom converted to office space. He said he didn't need much room for his type of work. It wasn't like he worked a lot of hours. He said there were plenty of rodents out there, but most people tried to take care of the problem themselves. He usually got called when they found it nearly impossible to take care of the problem.

We told John that we were checking out everyone that owned a white van. We asked if he stored his van when not working. He said he drives it most of the time, even when not working. Its cheap advertising and he can claim most of the miles on his taxes.

We asked if he keeps a record of the places that he services. He said, "I have a program on my computer that I keep records on." We asked if he could check to see if he had a record of ever doing any work at the two victim houses.

He punched in each address in the computer and got a hit on one. He set traps and went back to plug holes at the Anderson house. But it was about two years previously that he did it. We also asked if he had any part time help ever. He said he never had the need for help and it wasn't that profitable of a business. He said that it paid enough for him to live comfortably, as he was single and he inherited his house from his cousin. He had a cousin that died from an auto accident about five years earlier. He had been single too, and John was his only living relative. I noticed that John had his pen on the left side of his desk.

I had picked up a small toy mouse that was lying on his desk. He had several of them lying around. I asked him about that and he said he gives them out to kids at houses where he makes calls. I tossed it to John instead of setting it down. He caught it with his left hand. I asked him if he would write his name on a piece of paper for us. He said sure and grabbed some paper. He picked up the pen and wrote his name right-handed. I was still going to keep him on our suspect list. He was either right-handed or possibly ambidextrous, had a white van, and had easy access to rat poison. He would, of course, be at the bottom of the list.

We asked him if he could account for his whereabouts on the two nights of the murders. He asked the dates and looked on his computer. He explained that when he had no service calls on Saturdays, he spent those days and nights at his girlfriend's place. She lived in Neilsville, which is about a half hour drive from here. According to his computer he had no calls that day. So, he said that put him at his girlfriend's those nights. He gave us her name and phone number to collaborate everything.

We thanked John for his time and got back in our car. We didn't really suspect John to be our killer, but decided we had to leave him on our list. He was fairly young and in good shape to where he could overpower a person. We would need to see what his financial situation was. He pretty much worked part time at his business. And being the town mayor couldn't pay very much. I do know that he inherited his house and maybe some money with it.

We decided to break for lunch and plan our next stop for this afternoon. I asked Rob if he could check to see if there were any records of who might have installed the safes at both houses. It would have taken a carpenter to redo the floors to get them in.

After lunch we had five private van owners to check on. We had mapped out a sequence to follow so it would save a lot of driving back and forth.

First up is Jay Smith. Yes, his name is really Smith, he tells us when we get to his place. He lives on Heron Lake in a small house he inherited from his father. He has a wife named Susan who's a pretty little thing. He has a young son aged eight, who thinks it's cool to have the police at his house. Jay shows us the white van after we explain why we are there. He says the transmission is out of it, and he can't afford to fix it yet. You could tell it has sat for a while because of the grass growing all around it. We thank Jay and head to our next stop.

Next up is a Tony Clooney and his wife answers the door. We inform her of our reason for being there and she invites us in. She then explains that her husband Tony passed away about a year ago from an aneurism. She hasn't had time to sell the van yet, so it's just been sitting. We gave her our condolences and told her she might be able to make a deal with Jay Smith. We explained his needing a transmission and not having enough money for one. He could probably make one good van out of the two. They are the same model and only a year apart in age. So, the parts should be interchangeable. She thanked us and we left scratching her name off our list.

Our next stop was a guy named Jerome Freely. He lives just outside the town of Rosenwood. His place is a run-down trailer not far from the county dump. In fact, you drive by his house to get to the dump. Jerome didn't seem to be home and there was no white van in sight. We decided to check back after supper, thinking he probably had a job and was at work.

We had two more stops to check out yet. The first ended up being a dead end. The van was junk and just sitting there rotting away. White vans were not especially popular unless you own a business.

It was getting close to time for supper, or dinner for some people. We decided to break to go eat. We would check on Jerome Freely again at six thirty. Then we would check the last name on the list.

I stopped at the station to check for any messages before going to the diner. There was a message to call Joe Blaine in Madison.

I called Joe and got him just before he left for the night. He called to inform me that all the blood at the murder scene was from the decedents. The blood on the broken glass was also from the decedents. Also, all the fingerprints were from them too. There was no other trace evidence found at the scene. I thanked Joe and hung up. I just sat there for a while trying to collect my thoughts. These murders were too simple and quick. And the lack of evidence was hard to believe with all the blood. The killer had to get some blood on him or herself. There were footprints in the blood, but they had no form to them. It was like they had foot covers on. You can get foot covers pretty easily. The police crime investigators and hospital personnel have easy access to them. They are also available at other various places. Even car painters use them when spray painting.

I also hadn't forgotten the break-ins to my house and the similarities to the crime scenes. It made no sense at all.

I grabbed a sandwich at Barb's and went back to the station to tag up with Rob. We headed out to Jerome Freely's trailer house first.

There was a light on at his trailer and a white van in the driveway. I knocked on the door, and I heard someone in the rear of the trailer shout to hold on. We then heard a toilet flush so we relaxed a bit. A young man came to the door and asked gruffly what we wanted. He was a rough-looking guy about six foot two, and probably around 220 to 230 in weight. He needed a shave, haircut, and a shower. Even his clothes looked pretty ripe. We asked if he was Jerome Freely.

He says, "Who wants to know?"

I replied, "We're with the Black Crow police department, and we'd like ask you some questions."

He replied, "What if I don't want to answer them?" I told him we could take him in to the station, but that would waste his time and ours.

"We just want to ask a few questions about your van. I told him we were talking to anyone that owns a white van.

He said to go ahead and ask away. We asked where he had been last Saturday night. He thought for a minute and then said, "I was in Black River Falls all day and night. I was with a girlfriend and didn't come home until late Sunday afternoon." He gave us his girlfriend's name and phone number. I noticed that he wore a watch on his left hand making him right-handed. So, we thanked him and went on our way.

Our last van to check on belongs to a Jack Sampson. His place of residence was outside the town of Rosenwood. It took us about fifteen minutes to get there. The house was on a dirt lane. We pulled into it and looked for house numbers.

When we arrived, the place was dark. The sun was just going below the horizon. The house was the last one down the lane after two others places. We grabbed our flashlights and went to the front door. The house was completely without paint. There was trash piled all over the place. A dog started to bark inside the house as we came up the front steps. We knocked on the door but got no answer except for the dog going nuts. It jumped up on a window by the door and made us jump. It was a black faced German Shepard, and I'd say a male by the size of it. I hoped it wouldn't break through the window trying to get at us.

We descended the steps and decided to take a quick look around. I went one way around the house, and Rob went around the garage. After a minute Rob hollered to come behind the garage.

I quickly ran to Rob behind the garage to see a white van sitting there. We tried the doors but they were locked. We shined our lights through the windows but saw nothing. It looked as though the van had been moved lately as the grass was flattened down where the tires would make a path.

We decided to come back on Wednesday to try and catch Jack Sampson at home. We then jumped into the car and started driving back down the road.

Just as we got to the end of the road a car turned in front of us and headed down the road. We got the license plate number and called it in. I turned the car around and headed back down the road towards Sampson's place. We saw the car pull into Sampson's driveway. Just as we got there the call came through that the car belonged to Jack Sampson.

We pulled into the driveway just as Jack was headed to the house. I called out to the man asking if he was Jack Sampson. I identified us as the local police. All of a sudden, he draws a gun from behind his back and starts firing toward us. We ducked down behind our car and draw our weapons. I did notice that he fired the gun with his left hand.

Next thing we know he's jumping in his car and starts it. He fires back toward us again and then pulls around the garage heading for the back yard. We jump in our car and head after him.

The call we got saying it was Jack's van also told us that he owned a 1986 Ford Bronco. The Bronco headed through the backyard and into a sparse woods. There must be a dirt track back there that he knows about. We followed trying to catch up to him.

I'm driving, so Rob calls in to have dispatch get us some backup. We follow through the trees as best we can. The Bronco's taillights are still in view. After about half a mile. the trees clear and its open field.

The ground starts to get rougher and it's bouncing the car around pretty bad. If we didn't have seat belts on our heads would have been bouncing off the headliner.

It was pretty dark out now, and we didn't see the big deep gully come up. I should have suspected it because Sampson's Bronco had disappeared temporarily before that. Our car went down into it and the front end slammed into the other side.

Our airbags inflated smashing us back against the seats. After they deflated, I checked myself out feeling for any injuries. I asked Rob how he was. We both seemed to be okay, so Rob got on the radio and called in our situation.

He also told them to put out an APB for Jack Sampson and the Bronco. He also asked for a tow truck to get us out.

About half an hour later, the tow truck from Clancy's Service Station found us. He managed to get us pulled out, but not without a few chuckles. But once he saw the bullet holes in the car, he got more serious. He said it was the first time he had seen bullet holes in a vehicle.

On a preliminary examination of the car, Clancy said it looked like the frame might be bent. Once he got it to the shop, he'd be able to tell better. I told him it wasn't much of a loss as the car was on its last legs anyways. The three of us jammed into the cab of his truck and headed for town. Clancy dropped us off at the police station and said he'd let us know what he finds.

At the station we went right in to see Chief Turner and give him our report. After we filled him in, he said he would get a search warrant from the judge for Jack Sampson's house and garage. He also hoped to catch Jack and charge him with attempted murder and fleeing from the police. He was also a suspect in the double killings. Then we'd see what we could find at his house.

We had a couple cups of coffee while waiting for the warrant. We called into the Humane Society to see if someone could meet us at Sampson's house to get the dog out for us. When the warrant finally came through, we checked out another squad car. We seemed to get all the junk cars to use. Or maybe the town just couldn't afford newer vehicles. This car wasn't much better than the last one. Then we headed out for Sampson's house to check things out.

Once at the house, we lucked out. Sampson had already unlocked the door when we approached him earlier. The guy from the Humane Society who met us threw some meat in the door for the dog. The dog ate the meat and actually lay down to sleep. He then used a neck restraint he brought along to snare him. He said that he put some muscle relaxer in the meat to settle the dog down. He then took the dog away so we could then get in the house.

We opened the door and called out that we were from the police. When we got no answer, we walked in. The place was a real pigsty with empty food containers lying all over the kitchen. There was definitely no food to spoil lying around with that German Shephard living in there. He was huge and had to weigh in at least one hundred and twenty pounds.

We looked around the kitchen, doing a quick once-over. Mainly just opening up cabinet doors and drawers. We turned up nothing in the kitchen. Next, we moved to the dining room.

In the dining room there was a lot of junk setting around. Clothes and boxes full of junk. I think he was just too lazy to throw things out. There was more of the same in the living room. There were also more food containers lying around in there. They were pretty much all chewed up from the dog.

Next stop was upstairs. Here we hit the jackpot. The first bedroom was completely full of brand-new high-end stereos. It had to be a full truckload. The next bedroom was full of tools. It was mostly power tools from DEWALT. All brand-new in the boxes. It looked like another truckload. Obviously, this was all stolen merchandise. Probably from hijacked trucks that there were reports on throughout the state.

We moved next to the last bedroom up there. This bedroom had a bed and dresser in it. But the dresser had a bunch of small boxes setting on it. I opened a box and found it full of blank charge cards. It's no wonder that Jack Sampson ran. I would have taken off too if I was him.

We spent the next few hours searching the house and garage. We called the chief to see how he wanted to handle securing the scene. We let him know what we found and that there was no sign of jewelry or cash lying around. He did say there'd be an officer coming over to secure the scene. Then we could make some calls to see about reports on where the merchandise might have come from. It looked like a job for the state police or maybe even the FBI.

We figured we'd wait until morning to start working the case. The merchandise wasn't going anywhere. Plus, we were tired and needed to get some rest. I dropped Rob at the station so he could get his car. Then I headed home to get some sleep. I knew I would be sore all over in the morning from the accident.

I hit the shower and made it to my bed. Once in it I don't remember a thing as I passed out cold. But it didn't last long. I heard a phone ringing and hoped it was a dream. It just kept on ringing and wouldn't stop. Seeing as how I got to bed at about eleven o'clock and the clock now showed one o'clock, it was a short sleep.

I felt like I was drugged trying to wake up. I answered the phone to a very agitated Chief John Turner. He was quick to get to the point. There was another murder, and it was Willow Lake. He gave me the address and asked if I could pick up Rob on my way. I agreed to that and asked him to call him for me so he'd be ready.

I ran into the bathroom and filled the sink with ice cold water. I then dunked my head into it to shock myself awake. I then went to the kitchen and make some instant coffee in the microwave. Not the best tasting, but I was after the caffeine to help wake me.

I picked up Rob and headed to the murder scene. It was on Lake Street at the end of the block. Lake Street has only two other houses on it. The first house we went by was all dark. The other house was across the road from where the two police cars sat. The house across the street had lights on with a woman standing out on the porch.

The chief was waiting outside the house for us along with an elderly man who seemed to be distraught. The house was a cute little Swiss-style bungalow. It looked like a gingerbread house for a fairy tale. The area was wooded on both sides of the house with another street on the back side.

When we approached the chief, he introduced the man as John Sagget the owner of the house. He said when he got home, he went in and called for his wife (Betty), but got no answer. He then went upstairs and found her dead in their bed. He then called the police.

The man seemed upset but was very coherent and not a tear in his eyes. Normally a spouse is so grief-stricken that it's hard to get information out of them.

The chief said he already called Madison for a crime scene crew to work the scene. He also told us that the body was upstairs in the bedroom. He said the house and outside has been cleared and was safe to go in. So, Rob and I slipped on shoe covers and latex gloves before heading into the house.

Once inside we decided to check out the body first. We headed upstairs and as we got closer to the top you could smell copper. There was only one bedroom and what looked like a bathroom upstairs. Walking into the bedroom we could see a body on the bed. It was an older woman with gray hair. She was in her nightgown with red blood in a pool between her breasts. There wasn't blood everywhere like the other murders. After closer inspection it looked as if she had only been stabbed once. She must have died instantly stopping her heart. There was no blood spattered around, making it a pretty clean kill. She was lying down and didn't bleed out. The most blood was pooled around the insertion point. Some had run down the sides of her body. The blood had turned a very dark red, almost purple. So it had been some time since she was stabbed.

There was a glass sitting on the night stand that was just about empty. It looked clear and I took a sniff, but there was no smell, so I assumed it was water. We looked around, but everything seemed to be in order. The place was not ransacked, and we couldn't find a safe anywhere. There was a jewelry box on the dresser, and it was empty.

The rest of the house seemed normal, so we went back out to talk to Mr. Sagget. We asked if he had a safe anywhere in the house. He informed us he didn't, and he kept any important papers and any money in the bank.

I also asked about what time his wife usually went to bed. He said normally she went to bed around ten o'clock. But tonight she didn't feel well after supper, so she said she was going to bed early.

I asked him where he had been tonight. He said he played cards at the VFW on Wednesday nights. He left the house around six thirty. He arrived back home a little before midnight. I then asked if he had any enemies or had problems with anyone lately. He said he had no problems with anyone. He has been retired for about five years from the GM plant in Janesville. They moved up here to spend their last years relaxing after all their years of working. His wife, Betty, had been a nurse for forty years at various health organizations in southern Wisconsin.

The neighbor across the road seemed to be up, what with the flashing red and blue lights on the block. Rob and I decided to talk to the neighbor to see if they saw something.

We went across the road, and there was a woman standing on the porch. We introduced ourselves and she gave her name as Mrs. Irene Hood. She is widowed and said she has lived in her house for the last twenty-five years. She told me that Betty and John had moved in across the street about four or five years ago. She said Betty always sat out on their front porch on the evenings that John would go out. Tonight, was different, though. Betty did not sit out on the porch tonight. She figured maybe Betty was sick.

She said that she was on her porch when John left tonight and called hello to him. But he completely ignored her and seemed in a hurry. She said he normally acknowledges her when she says hello.

I asked if Betty and John seemed to get along okay. She said John seemed to be pretty controlling and she had heard arguing once in a while over there. Mrs. Hood said she talked to Betty quite a bit, but she never mentioned any problems.

I thanked Mrs. Hood and wished her a good night. We walked down to the other house to see if anyone was around. We knocked, but the house seemed to be deserted. There was so much mail built up that it overflowed the mailbox. Apparently, no one had been here for a while.

We went back to the chief to let him know what we found out.

While we were talking, the crime scene crew form Madison pulled up. We gave them a quick briefing of what we knew so they could get started.

I informed the chief that there wasn't much I could do tonight and was going to go get a little sleep. I didn't figure I could do much good being so tired. I said I'd be in early and get the crime scene crew's report. I took the chief off to the side and told him this was much different than the other murders. I was going to sleep on it and I'd talk to him in the morning.

I had a hunch that was lurking in the back of my mind. I didn't want to say anything yet until I had time to think it over. I also wanted to get home to make sure my house hadn't been broken into.

When I arrived home, everything seemed to be the same way I left it, so I jumped back in bed and after rolling some ideas around in my head I finally fell asleep.

Chapter 16

. . . .

June 20 Wednesday Morning

I woke up at six thirty to a bright sunny morning. The sun was streaming in through the window. I crawled out of bed and hit the shower. My mind had been racing about the new murder until I finally fell asleep in the early morning hours. Now it was crowded again with a million questions. What little I knew about the murder didn't make sense. I stopped at Barb's diner for a quick coffee and roll to tide me over. Barb said word was out about the killing last night. That's why the diner was pretty dead this morning.

"People are starting to worry about how safe they are," she said. "This is a lot of crime for such a small community."

I made it to the police station by seven thirty and found Rob waiting for me in the conference room. I think both of our minds seemed much clearer this morning. There's nothing like a little sleep to make the day look better. He had a copy of the medical report from the coroner. I did a quick read of the report to see what we had. There was nothing that stood out in it. The depth of the stab wound seemed to indicate the knife was probably about nine or ten inches long. That sounds a lot like a kitchen knife possibly. Not the same length as the other killings. The medical examiner figured those were made by a knife about six to eight inches, like a hunting knife.

I started out by telling Rob this murder doesn't have any similarities to the other killings. We never put out all of the details of the first two murders. We withheld some of the facts to avoid possible copycats.

For one thing there was no broken glass in any doors at this murder scene. The electricity was not turned off and they had no safe or great amount of money in the house. Plus, it was just the single killing and not a couple.

There was some jewelry missing, but it didn't seem like that much. It definitely wasn't enough to kill someone over. I told Rob that we should get the chief in and run some things by him.

So Rob went looking for the chief while I called Jane. We had a date to go out for dinner tonight, and I figured we might be busy. We needed to come up with some answers on these crimes. I figured we needed to start from the beginning and review and re-interrogate everyone. It was going to be a long day. I knew she wouldn't be happy about it but would understand.

Rob came back with the chief and I told Rob to shut the door. The chief asked if we had any new leads in the cases. I informed him of the difference in this last case compared to the others. My idea was to pull John Sagget in for questioning.

The first person of interest is usually the spouse. We didn't really question him much last night thinking it was related to the other murders. But my gut says that the husband could be a good suspect.

I asked the chief about pulling John Jones in for questioning and maybe getting a search warrant for his house and vehicle. The chief thought it was a good idea but that we should probably wait until we could get a search warrant. We needed to have more proof to show the judge if we wanted a search warrant for everything. But we needed to dig into all of the Jones's records that we could get access to.

"I'm going to call his girlfriend now to see if she can provide an alibi for him," I said.

We broke the meeting up and I headed for a phone. I dialed the number John Jones gave me and got an answer on the second ring. I told her my name and that I was with the Black Crow police department. I asked if this was Megan Myers and she said it was. I asked if she knew John Jones. She answered she did and has for quite a while.

I then asked if she could verify that John had been with her on the two nights of the killings. She replied that she had been with him the last four Saturdays in a row. I asked if it was all night for those two weekends. She said they'd fallen asleep watching television on all four Saturdays, and he was there in the morning. It was pretty much the same routine every weekend. Nothing had changed from this routine lately. I thanked her and hung up. John Jones seemed to be a dead end, but I was still keeping him on the list.

So, Rob and I spent Thursday and Friday recanvassing the areas around all three crime scenes. We came up with nothing new at any of the crime scenes. The only thing we accomplished was to burn up some shoe leather.

Chapter 17

. . . .

June 22 Saturday Morning

I got to the station around eight o'clock to find Rob and the chief waiting for me. There was also a man in a suit with them. His demeanor and general appearance seemed to say cop to me. He stuck his hand out for me to shake and introduced himself as Cory Miller. The chief said he was an insurance investigator for the New Life Insurance Company. He told us all to have a seat and let Mr. Miller fill us in on his reason for being here.

Once we were seated Mr. Miller said to call him Cory. He said, "I've been sent by our head office to investigate the Betty Sagget killing. We automatically investigate anytime the policy is a million dollars or more. John Sagget took out a one-million-dollar policy on his wife a little over a year ago. So, before we pay out, I have to make sure everything is on the up and up. I would appreciate any facts you can give me to satisfy our records.

"I'm kind of curious, Cory. Sagget's wife just died a few days ago. You're saying someone called in already about collecting on the insurance policy? Or did you just hear about this on the news?"

"That's an interesting question Mr. Moran. According to my records I have here that the call came in on Wednesday from Mr. Sagget personally. It's very unusual for someone to call in that soon unless it's the police investigating."

"You can call me Duke, and I can tell you that we are checking into this killing. This info you just gave us shines some new light into things. If you can hang around for the rest of the day, we might have some answers for you a little later."

"I appreciate any help you can give, and if you'll excuse me, I'll go for some breakfast. Is there any place you can recommend for a decent breakfast?"

"Yes, I eat at Barb's Diner downtown. It doesn't get any better than her food and service."

"That sounds good, and I see you have a nice peaceful looking park down on the square. It looks like a good place for me to relax and maybe get some paperwork done. I also have plenty of phone calls to make. Here's my card with my cell phone number on it. I'll look forward to hearing from you later."

After Cory left, we sat back down to digest what we'd just learned. The chief figured we had enough for a search warrant now. We don't need a search warrant for the house because it's a murder scene. But we do need one for his car and to check bank records, plus any other personal items we need to check out. He said to give him about an hour to get the warrant and set up some deputies to do the search while we question Mr. Sagget.

We found out that John Sagget had gotten a room at the Lazy Tree Motel because the house was sealed as a crime scene. So Rob and I headed out to pick him up. We could have called him and asked him to come in. But I thought it would be a better idea to go get him. I didn't want to give him a heads-up and have him taking off.

It was almost noon, so I hoped he was still in his room. We pulled up to the office at the Lazy Tree Motel, and I sent Rob in to get the room number. Rob came back and said John Sagget was in room number eighteen, which is in the rear.

As we pull around the building, we see a young woman coming out of room eighteen. She came out and got in a red Ford Mustang convertible and drove off. She was dressed in a very sexy red dress. The dress didn't hide much and left little to the imagination. Rob and I looked at each other and both said wow. But you never know, maybe it was his daughter. But I found that hard to believe especially since she was stuffing what looked like money into her purse on the way to her car.

We went up to the door and knocked. John Sagget opened the door and looked surprised to see us. He knew who we were so there was no reason to reintroduce ourselves.

We said we had some more questions we needed to ask him and could he come with us to the station. He said he would rather drive himself, but we insisted he come with us. He reluctantly came with us after we told him he'd get a ride back.

We got back to the station and took him back to the stockroom, which is the only private place we had to do the interview. We had put a small table in there with three chairs. We got John seated and asked if he wanted something to drink. He asked for some water, and Rob went to get it. I asked John if he minded my recording our talk and he kind of balked at that. I informed him that he was not under arrest, and we were just gathering information. Plus, it was for his protection as well as ours. When I told him that, he said the recording was all right.

We had set it up so the chief would call us out for some phony reason. We wanted to give John some time to sit and think. But also to give the deputies the chief sent to search the house time to find something. Hopefully they could find something while we had him at the station.

After about half an hour we decided to start the questioning. Rob and I went in and apologized to Mr. Sagget for the wait. We explained that we got some of the preliminary results back from the crime lab. He seemed to be getting agitated and was having a hard time sitting still. He was starting to sweat also.

I asked if he would like some more water to drink. He said some water would help. We had decided to start out easy and try to gain Sagget's confidence. As Rob left to get the water, I asked if he managed any sleep last night. He replied that he went to a motel for the night but had a hard time trying to sleep. I could see how he might have had a hard time sleeping.

Rob got back with the water, and Sagget drank down about three quarters of it right away. I told him we needed to get our time line straightened out for last night.

I asked him to run through everything he did yesterday up until he got home last night. He said he got up at about eight o'clock in the morning, and Betty made him breakfast. Then he spent most of the morning servicing the lawn mower and eventually mowing the lawn. After lunch he took a couple hours' nap. Next, he washed the car and just messed around in the garage doing some cleaning and organizing things until dinner. He said Betty had made a pot roast for dinner and after eating, she cleaned up while he watched a game show on television. He then left for the VFW at about six thirty.

I asked Sagget how his wife and he got along. He replied, "We are, or I mean, we were just as much in love as the day we got married. We would have the occasional argument over normal daily problems. Probably the same as most other married people. We were going to celebrate our forty-first anniversary next month. We had been planning a trip to California to celebrate it."

When asked about what jewelry was taken, he seemed to hesitate. He claimed there really wasn't much." There was the diamond ring from her mother and some other pieces she left her. Plus the few assorted pieces she had purchased since they had married. We never had any of it appraised because we didn't think it was worth that much."

I then asked if he found anything else missing in the house when the crime crew from Madison had him go through the house. This was of course after the body had been removed. He said everything seemed to be there from what he could see.

Rob then asked Sagget if he had noticed any strangers or people he didn't usually see in the neighborhood around lately. Also, if there were any odd vehicles coming around. Without having to even think, Sagget said, "I haven't seen any strange people, but had seen a white van drive through occasionally lately.

I realized at that moment that word was out about our checking on people with white vans. As fast as Sagget answered, I figured that was where he got that from.

I was starting to have some very serious doubts about this guy. I noticed that Rob seemed to be sending out the same signals about him. We had Sagget sign a form saying he had been read his rights. It was mainly a ploy to see which hand he wrote with. He signed it with his left hand.

I next asked Sagget, "Who was the lovely lady we saw exiting your motel room when we pulled up this morning?"

That question stopped him instantly. You could just see his mind racing to come up with an answer. The sweat also started to run down the side of his face. He had to use the sleeves of his shirt to stop the sweat from running into his eyes.

With a stutter he replied, "She was delivering food to me."

I asked who delivered breakfast around here. I hadn't heard of any restaurant delivering breakfast around our area.

He answered, "She is a friend of ours and called to see if I'd like her to bring some food over. I was hungry, so I thanked her and she brought it over."

So I answered, "If we go over to your motel room, we're going to find the remnants of your breakfast sitting there or in the trash?"

He said, "You have no right to go into my room without my permission."

My reply was, "We have every right. I can get a search warrant just like the one we have for your house that's being checked right now. The first suspect in the death of a spouse is the other spouse. Once we have a time of death for your wife and verify your timeline, we can eliminate you as a suspect."

About this time there's a knock on the door and the chief sticks his head in and asks to see me. I excused myself and along with Rob we left the room.

We went to the chief's office and he told me shut the door and then take a seat. He had one call from the officers checking out the Sagget house. They had found nothing incriminating so far. But they did find ten thousand dollars in a lock box in the desk. Also, there was a life insurance policy on both John Sagget and his wife for thirty thousand dollars each. The policies were about twenty years old. That didn't seem like enough money to kill over.

I had also told the search team ahead of time to look for any bloody clothes. They said when they called in that there was a small load of men's clothes in the washing machine. They had already gone through the full cycle. So that would be of no use.

While we were still in the chief's office, the office clerk knocked and said she had just received the Madison investigator crews report on the fax machine. I took it from her and scanned the pages quickly. Everything was pretty normal except for one thing.

They had checked for any missing knives, but couldn't tell because all the knives were just dumped in a drawer. But they did find blood residue in the kitchen sink drain trap. That's not abnormal, but they took a sample to check out. They also said they had checked all the knives for any blood residue that could be human. They did find residue on one knife.

Come to find out it was human blood and it was O positive. That was the same as the victim's type. They were going to do a DNA test on it. But that would take at least a couple of weeks to get results on.

We all had the feeling that this murder was not associated with the other two. It was time to put the pressure on Sagget. So all three of us headed back to the stockroom where Sagget was being held.

When we went back in the interrogation room, John Sagget was very agitated and white as a ghost. I asked if he was okay. He replied that he didn't feel very well and needed to go back to bed.

I asked if maybe it was something he ate for breakfast. He just glared at me and said it was from being cooped up in this tiny room. I asked Rob to go get some towels for Mr. Sagget as he was sweating profusely. The table we were at was actually getting wet from his sweating. It wasn't that hot in the room so something was bothering him. Well, it wasn't going to get any better for him.

I started out by asking, "Mr. Sagget, I find it difficult to believe that your house was broken into, your wife killed, and all that was taken is some jewelry. We have a search warrant for your house and they found ten thousand dollars in your desk drawer. Also, none of the house was ransacked. Doesn't this seem a bit odd to you?"

"You have no right to search my house. Why are you wasting time questioning me and searching my house instead of looking for my wife's killer? I want a lawyer right now and I'm not answering anymore questions."

"We're just trying to get a timeline on what happened and where everyone was yesterday. This is standard procedure in cases like this. We're trying to find out who else might have means and motive to break into your house. You're not under arrest. This is just an information gathering session. If you feel you need a lawyer, then that is your right."

"You're damn right it's my right, and I want one now. I feel like your interrogating me for something I didn't do and I'm not going to stand for it."

By now Mr. Sagget is shaking all over and the sweat is running off him like a faucet, turned on wide open. I try to calm him down, but he's completely lost control. All of a sudden, he grabs his chest and falls out of his chair.

My first guess is he's having a heart attack. I holler at Rob to call 9-1-1 and get the paramedics here. I unbutton his shirt and loosen his belt. He's still breathing, but it's labored.

The paramedics arrive in about five minutes. They hook him up to oxygen and start getting his vitals. Then they get him on a gurney and wheel him out to their van and whisk him off to the hospital.

Meanwhile, we sat around scratching our heads trying to make some sense of what just happened. It's obvious that Jones is probably guilty. He had the motive, which was money and the arguments heard between him and his wife. And having the means and opportunity are obvious. He tried to make it look like the other two murders, but he didn't know all the facts from the other ones.

I figured I should fill the chief in on what happened at my house after the two murders. I informed him of the broken glass in my back door just like at the murder scenes. And that my electricity was turned off also.

The chief was as baffled as Rob and myself on that one. He said we had to get a break on these cases soon or else we'd have to get the state more involved.

While we're contemplating our next move, Judy, the dispatcher on duty came in. She said, "A call just came in from the hospital. They said Mr. Sagget was checked into the emergency room twenty minutes ago, and has just disappeared. After they took his vitals, he was left alone waiting for a doctor to see him. When the doctor went to check on him his bed was empty."

The hospital in Black Crow is very small. It's more like a large clinic. They mostly take care of small accidents and ailments. Anything big is taken to Black River Falls Hospital. So there is no security at the hospital to secure the exits.

The chief told Judy to let the hospital know that we would go look for him. The chief turned to us and said, "Get out there and find Sagget, and when you do, lock him up."

I figured the best place to start was his house. So Rob and I headed there. We pulled up in front of the Sagget house. It was about two o'clock and the neighborhood was pretty quiet. There is a car in the driveway, and I am guessing it belongs to Sagget. He must have gone right to the motel to pick it up. I call in the plate number to be sure.

As Rob and I get out of the car, we hear glass breaking from the house. The house is set back about five hundred feet from the street. All of a sudden there is a shot and it hits the front fender of the car. Rob and I duck behind the car.

I sneak a look up at the house and see some movement in the upstairs window. Then we hear Sagget yelling at us, "Get out of here and leave me alone. I'm not answering anymore questions from you."

I noticed the shot was from a pistol, so chances of getting hit were slim. It's hard to be accurate at the distance we are from the house unless the person is an expert sharpshooter.

I ask Rob if he has a megaphone in the car. He says there's one in the trunk. I open the driver side door and get the keys. Then I sneak around to the trunk and open it. I then grab the megaphone so I can speak to Sagget.

I ask Mr. Sagget to come down so we can talk and straighten this all out. He yelled back that he was done talking. He said, "I know you're trying to railroad me for all the murders going on plus my wife's."

All of a sudden, he gets off two more rounds into the car. When I look back up, there is smoke coming from the upstairs window where he had fired from. I don't see him in the window, so I decide to rush the house.

I tell Rob to cover me and call the fire department as soon as I get up there. I take off running for the front door. I make the porch safely and check the front door. The door is locked so I throw my weight into it to bust it open. It takes a couple of tries but finally gives way and I go tumbling in. I guess I need to start working out.

I see the stairway down the hallway. It's down from me towards the kitchen. I move towards the stairway keeping my gun, which I have drawn, aimed up the stairs. Smoke is starting to fill the upstairs hallway now. I quickly run up the stairs, taking them two at a time. I reach the top and see no one, so I go to the front bedroom.

I see the bed is on fire, which is where his wife was killed. Sagget is nowhere in sight, and the fire has spread to the curtains and the walls. I back track and check the remaining bedroom and the bathroom. Both are empty, so I head back down stairs.

I hear the sirens of the fire department in the distance. I do a quick check of the living room, dining room, and downstairs kitchen. I head to the kitchen and see the back door is hanging open. I carefully go out and there is no one in sight. All the backyards run up to each other the whole block long. As I go out in the yard, I notice someone looking out the window from the house behind.

I wave for them to come out. It's a young woman that looks to be in her midtwenties. She's a cute, slender lady with mousy brown short hair.

We meet at the property line of the yards, and I introduce myself. She tells me her name is Miranda Hays.

I ask if she saw anyone go through the backyards in the last ten minutes. She says, "I heard what I thought was either a shot or lawn mower backfiring. I looked out the kitchen window but saw nothing. Then shortly after that I heard two more bangs similar to the first one. I looked out the window again and saw Sagget run out of his back door and go between our garage and the neighbor's house. I see there's smoke coming from his house. Are we safe here or should I get my daughter out and leave the area?"

I said, "You should be okay. The fire department is here and should have it under control shortly." I thanked her and headed back to Rob.

When I got back in front of the Sagget house and found Rob, the chief had arrived. I filled both of them in on what I knew. The chief got on the radio to the dispatcher to get all officers in and on duty. And put out an APB to the surrounding area for John Sagget.

Now we have two people on the run that we're looking for. We still haven't found Jack Sampson either. You'd think it should be easy to find someone here, but it's not. Between the three towns and lakes there are about twenty-five hundred people. That's if all the summer people are here. At any given time, a lot of the houses are unoccupied on the lakes. Plus, when you throw in all the wooded acreage, there are plenty of places to hide. And we only have a handful of people to do a decent search.

So as soon as everybody was assembled in the main room of the station, we handed out pictures of John Sagget. We had sent an officer to the Sagget house to get a picture of him. We informed everyone that John Sagget had been brought in for questioning about the death of his wife. We thought he was having a heart attack so we sent him to the hospital. He then disappeared from there and was found at his house. When we approached his house, he opened fire on us. Then he started the house fire and escaped through the backyards.

The chief then addressed everyone. "Our job today is finding Mr. Sagget and taking him into custody as a suspect in the murder of his wife. He is armed and dangerous, so if you find him call for backup. Do not try to apprehend him yourself. We also gave you a fact sheet on Mr. Sagget. It has a rough idea of his height and weight. There is also a description of his car and the license number. We will now hand out the areas for each group to search. So good luck and be careful out there."

John and I jumped in our replacement vehicle and headed to our section, which is by Crabs Lake over at Chaney. There are not many houses on or around Crabs Lake. It's mostly country roads and some aren't even paved. We covered every road in our assigned area and then decided to talk to some of the people to see if they saw anything. We stopped at several houses and questioned the people about anyone strange hanging around. Everyone said it was a pretty quiet Saturday.

We were about ready to give up here when we got a call on the radio. A Tom Phelps, who has a small farm out by Willow Lake called in about ten minutes ago. He saw a man run into his old barn. When he ran outside and called out to the man, he was shot at. He said the guy was either a lousy shot or was just firing a warning shot because he missed him by a country mile.

We got the address and headed to the place. It was out on Skunk Road, which is around a mile from Crabs Lake. We arrived to find two other squad cars there parked out on the road. The chief was there hunkered down behind one of the cars. We joined him to find out the situation. He said Mr. Phelps was in the house. Phelps is the owner of the farm.

We could see a car parked in the ditch farther down the road. My guess was that it was probably stolen by Sagget in making his getaway. He must have run out of gas or broke down to have stopped out here. We still weren't sure if it was Sagget in the barn. But seeing as how he was armed and not afraid to shoot, it was probably him.

The farm was situated right along the road. The area was wooded all around the buildings. It had a wide-open area between the house and barn. I suggested that I go around through the woods behind the house and talk to Mr. Phelps to get a layout of the barn and surrounding area. Chief Turner said to go ahead, and if Sagget started firing, they would cover for me.

So off I went through the trees and came out behind the house. I had to go around the back side of the house to find a door. It was an old two-story farmhouse that was in bad need of painting.

I knocked on the door and called as quietly as possible to Mr. Phelps. I identified myself as a police officer and flashed my old police ID to him. He then opened the door and let me in. So far, no more shots had been fired.

Mr. Phelps took me to the side of the house facing the barn. It was a huge barn that was slowly falling apart. The barn lay parallel to the road. There was a hay door on the upper level that was hanging open and it faced the house. Underneath it was an open area that went under the barn. It had wire fencing all around it. I thought I saw some movement in the fenced area. I asked Mr. Phelps what was in that area and what was behind it.

He said it was a pig pen with twenty-five hogs in it. I could see some of them moving around in there and could definitely hear them grunting and squealing. Mr. Phelps said they were probably hungry because it was past feeding time.

He said the back of the barn was full of old machinery. The haymow was mostly empty except for a few bales of hay he used as bedding for the hogs. He informed me that the hog pen was pretty muddy. He had been keeping it watered down to keep the hogs cool. He didn't recommend going in it because it would be hard to keep standing. The fact is that the hogs get pretty ornery when their hungry. It could be downright dangerous to go in there. He did say there was another door on the side opposite the road. To get in the haymow there are two ladders either side of the barn on the inside.

I called the chief and filled him in the layout. While I was talking to him, another squad car pulled up. When that happened, Sagget started shooting towards the squads. He got about four shots off, and the chief and other officers returned fire. I could see Sagget up in the upper hay door, and he jumped back when he was fired upon. I could have fired at him, but I was afraid of him firing back and possibly hitting Mr. Phelps.

I told the chief that I was going to try and work my way around to the back side of the barn and go in that door. He gave me the go ahead and said they would try to work their way to the door on the road side.

I snuck out the back of Mr. Phelps's house, back into the woods. I worked my way around through the woods to the back side of the barn. The back door wasn't even there. It had fallen off its hinges years ago, by the looks of it. I called in to Sagget to drop his weapon and come out with his hands up. I informed him who I was and that he was surrounded.

I got no answer and it was dead silence in the barn. So I decided to peek in and make sure the first floor was empty. It looked clear, so I crept in keeping an eye on the two openings above the ladders on each side. I decided to go over to the ladder on the front side of the barn. I figured he would be watching the ladder on the back side because I had called to him from there.

I reached the front ladder all right and started to climb it. This was the touchy part because I had to stick my head up through the floor to get a look up there. I could see some bales of hay on one side of the opening up above. This gave me some protection on one side. I stuck my head up through and got a quick look. It was all clear that way. I then looked the other way over the hay bales and saw nothing.

He wasn't up here, and then I got worried that he might be in the back part of the barn where the machinery was. I was a clear target for him up on this ladder. I quickly jumped up on the mow floor to get clear of the first floor.

I then ran over to the front of the barn to the mow door to warn the chief and other officers. There was only one officer at the squad cars, and I asked where the others were. He said they were just entering the front barn door.

I then hollered down to them that Sagget was not up in the mow. I said he might be down in the machinery at the back of the barn.

I then climbed back down to join them. We spread out and moved toward the rear of the barn with our weapons drawn and ready. We called out a warning for Sagget to come out peaceably. There was no answer, and it was just too quiet in there.

We kept advancing into the machinery and made it to the back of the barn. There was no one left in this barn. But we found some boards missing on the wall at the back. We guessed that Sagget must have got out this way. That meant the woods needed to be searched.

The woods went on for about a quarter of a mile. Then there was some field and then woods again. We were going to need more men for this. We went back to the squad cars to call in for more help. Skunk Road was about three miles long with no other farms or houses on it. It got its name for a very good reason. And it was the same reason no one lived on it. The nearest place was probably four or five miles away.

We were back at the squads with the chief on the radio calling for more help. All of a sudden, we heard shooting coming from down the road. It sounded like an AR-15 assault rifle being fired as fast as the trigger could be pulled. It was less than a mile, which didn't make any sense. There was nothing down that way.

We jumped in our squads and took off that way. We got down the road at about a mile when all of a sudden Sagget comes running out the tree line. He's screaming at the top of his lungs and waving his rifle around in the air.

We drew our weapons and shouted for him to put his weapon down. He was out of his mind and kept raving like he had lost his mind. He finally threw his rifle down hollering that he was out of bullets.

His face was drenched and he was having a hard time breathing. His eyes were all wet and running as well as his nose and mouth. As we got closer, we got a whiff of him and stopped in our tracks. We actually started to back up from the smell. We ordered Sagget to get down on the ground with his hands on the back of his head. He screamed that he couldn't breathe. We ordered him down on the ground and he finally got down.

He finally started to calm down a little and we asked what happened. He said he was running and fell over a tree root. Then all of a sudden, he was surrounded by ten to fifteen skunks. He said they all started to spray him at once.

He managed to get back up and more skunks were spraying him as he ran. He emptied his rifle trying to kill as many as he could.

The road got its name because for some odd reason there are a lot of skunks in the area. There is no way to tell how many skunks are actually in the area as it's hard to get someone to count them. But I've heard it could be hundreds. They're mostly confined to this last mile of the road. The road gets very little traffic because no one wants to take the chance of hitting one. They don't bother Mr. Phelps farm because they don't like the pig smell. It's hard to believe as bad as they smell themselves.

Nobody even uses the fields around here for crops anymore. I heard from some of the old farmers that at harvest time, this whole area smelled of skunk. The farmers would get sprayed plus their equipment also. So nobody farms the land around here anymore. The fields have gotten overgrown with weeds.

So here we are with Sagget so full of skunk oil that we can't get near him. Nobody wants him in their squad, but we have to get him somewhere to be cleaned up. We sure as hell can't put him in a cell like this or even transport him in a vehicle.

I mentioned to the chief about getting either a pickup truck or stock truck to haul him. Then we needed somewhere outside where we could spray him down.

The chief got ahold a buddy of his that has an old farm truck with high stake sides that he very seldom uses. I suggested that they bring some plastic shopping bags and tape. We can have Sagget put his hands and feet into the bags so he doesn't get the skunk oil on everything.

I then suggested taking him to the car wash in town. They have warm water that we can spray him down with. We also need some fresh clothes for him as we will need to throw his away. I said I'd go downtown to get what we needed to clean Sagget up.

The chief asked what would work to get the smell off Sagget. I said we can mix hydrogen peroxide, baking powder and dishwashing soap together. Then Sagget can wash down using a sponge with the solution. The mixture converts the skunk musk into an odorless chemical. It will probably take a couple of applications to get it off him. The chief said, "Let's go for it. The owner of the car wash might give us some grief about it, but I'll handle it. I'll tell him that the town will pay him enough to make it worth his while.

So I left and hit the hardware and grocery store to get everything we needed. By the time I got to the car wash they had Sagget there. I mixed up a bucket of the solution and put it in one of the wash bays. They got Sagget in there and had him strip down. We set him down with a hose and then instructed him to use the sponge and wash down with the solution. We then sprayed him down and did the process one more time.

When done and he got dried off, we gave him some old clothes and shoes we found for him. It seemed to have worked because when he walked out, he didn't seem to smell. Or else we were just getting used to the smell. He said his eyes were burning and he had a sore throat. So on the way to the police station I stopped and got some eyewash for him.

At the station they took Sagget back to the interrogation room/stockroom. It was a little crowded in the room. There was the chief, myself, and Rob.

Rob read Mr. Sagget his Miranda rights and told him he was under arrest for fleeing the police, endangering the lives of others by shooting at them, and attempted murder of the police officers, and private residents.

He said he ran because we were trying to railroad him for the murder of his wife and the other two couples that were killed. He said, "I would never kill my wife. I was deeply in love with her. We had a perfect marriage and were completely dedicated to each other."

I replied, "Why is it, then, that you were heard by others in the neighborhood as talking down to your wife and browbeating her?"

Sagget replied, "She needed to be told what to do all the time. She couldn't do anything on her own. I think sometimes she did things just to piss me off. She wasn't the brightest person in the world."

I said, "Your trying to tell us that a woman who was a registered nurse for forty years couldn't figure things out herself? Having to take care of people and do all the duties that nurses have to do. I would say her job was a lot tougher than putting the same part on a car all day. I think she was probably a saint for having to put up with you all these years."

That got to Sagget, and he came out of his chair at me yelling that I was calling him stupid. He said, "That stupid cow needed a man like me to control her life. Without me she couldn't survive. Anybody can do what nurses do. Anybody can cleanup for those doctors. There nothing more than glorified candy stripers."

"Well, Mr. Sagget, I can't believe your wife stayed with you all these years. You must have had her brainwashed. Can you tell me why you took out a life insurance policy for one million dollars on your wife, but you did not take one out for yourself? And it's odd that she was killed one year and seven days from when you took the policy out. It would not pay out until after you had it for at least a year. That's one hell of a coincidence."

"I took the policy out on just her because I figured she would die before me. She worked with all those sick people all those years. With all the diseases she was exposed to, I figured she would catch one of them and die. But she proved to be tougher than I thought."

"So is that why you killed her because you figured she might outlive you?"

"I didn't kill her. It had to be the same person that killed those other people. I had no reason to kill my wife. I was in love with her."

"You have a funny way of showing your love. You obviously didn't have any respect for your wife with the way you talk about her. She obviously was much smarter than you, and I think you felt inferior to her. We're also liking you for the other murders that have occurred lately. So we need to know your whereabouts on the evening of Saturday, June 8 and Saturday, June 17."

"I was at home on both those nights. We never went anywhere on Saturday nights. We didn't tend to socialize with people as a couple much. I spent some time at the VFW because I was a veteran, and it got me out of the house. I had to have a break once in a while from having to put up with Betty."

"Well, since we don't have your wife to corroborate your alibi, we'll have to check with your neighbors to see if they can verify it. But it's really suspicious about the timing on the life insurance. And for being such a loving couple, you don't have much good to say about your wife. It would be to your advantage to be up front with us now. The district attorney might be more forgiving if you tell the truth now. Your wife's murder has details that don't match up with the other murders.

"I would recommend you get a lawyer right away. We definitely have you on the charges we have already informed you of. Plus, charges will be forthcoming on the death of your wife."

"I have no more to say. I'm innocent and I'm done talking until I get a lawyer."

"Rob, can you take Mr. Sagget to call his lawyer and then lock him up in a nice tight cell. Make sure he's comfortable because he's going to be here for a while."

After Rob took Sagget away, the chief asked what the next step should be. I said, "We have enough evidence I think to bring Sagget back with his lawyer.

It would be nice to get him to confess. We have means, motive and possibly the weapon. He definitely had the means. He was possibly at home when she was killed. The coroner gave a time frame of five to eight o'clock. And there are plenty of knives in the house he could have used. He would have plenty of time to clean up afterwards.

"He definitely had motive. There was the one-million-dollar life insurance policy. And it was an awful big coincidence that she got killed right after the one year waiting period. Plus, he definitely didn't think much of his wife. What with the comments he made to us about her.

"We can tell him that all the knives have been looked at by the Madison crime lab. They believe there is blood residue on one of the knives found in the kitchen. Plus, they found blood residue in the kitchen drain. We can tell him that they have determined its human blood; they can then do DNA testing on it. It's already been determined it's the same blood type as his wife. This DNA testing is relatively new but has been proven to be infallible in matching whose blood is whose. We should have a search warrant to get a DNA sample from him just in case he won't do it voluntary.

"I don't think we have quite enough to arrest him and go to court yet. Hopefully the lab will come through with some good news soon. But for now, I think it's worth a try to get a confession. We could offer him a lesser charge than first degree murder. Maybe we could offer voluntary manslaughter. With that he would still probably die in prison."

The chief thought it sounded like a good idea to try. He said he would get the search warrant for a DNA sample and then set up the interview. "We might have to wait until Monday if I can't get Judge Harley. I'll see if he's at home, but being as its seven o'clock, I doubt we'll find him tonight. Hopefully he's staying home this weekend so maybe I can get him tomorrow. He likes to take off fishing if the weather is right."

"We can hold him for forty-eight hours, can't we? We have him on the other charges, which should be enough. He can't make bail on the weekend anyways because the courthouse is closed."

"That's right, Duke, so at the very least we have until Monday to get the warrant. We could also use these three charges we have on him as another bargaining chip. Hopefully his lawyer is a little lax. and we can sweat Sagget some. I think without the lawyer, it could be done. Look how shook up he got when we questioned him the first time."

"I agree it's a good plan. I'm going to take off. I'm starving and need to eat. We missed out on lunch and it's been a long day. So I'll talk to you tomorrow."

I left and called Jane up to see if she had eaten yet. She said she had not, but could use some food. I suggested meeting at Jack's Supper Club in Rosenwood. I said a steak and beer sounds wonderful to me. Jane agreed and said she'd be right there.

I got to the supper club first so I ordered us both a bottle of Spotted Cow. When she arrived, I suddenly felt more awake. She had that effect on me whenever I saw her. And she always smells great. No matter what time of the day it is. She wears this terrific cologne that seems to be made just for her. I stood up when she approached and gave her a big hug and kiss. I said that maybe we should skip eating and get on to the best part of the night. But I regretted that if I didn't eat soon, I'd probably pass out on her. We put our order in for food and then I filled her in on my day. Jane was surprised I hadn't fallen asleep yet. She said something to the effect of my getting old.

I replied that I would show her who was old after we got through eating. Jane said we'd better rush our meal and get going so I wouldn't fall asleep on her. She was smiling when she said it. Our meal came and I pretty much vacuumed my meal down.

We left the restaurant and went to Jane's apartment. She lives in the town of Chaney in an apartment above a garage. Don't get the wrong idea. It's a second garage behind a mini mansion. It's a beautiful apartment, and the garage is hers to use. There's actually a small elevator in the garage to take you up. That's how swanky the place is. The driveway is all brick and the garage floor is an epoxy finish with colored specks in it. The walls are covered with cedar siding. The windows even had curtains in them.

The apartment inside is a very comfortable open space. The living room has a triple patio door that goes out on a deck. It looks out over Crabs Lake to the east. The sunrise in the morning is awesome to see. I was hoping to see in the coming morning. The ceilings have wood beams running across them and all the floors are hardwood made of Alder. And in the bedroom, there is a skylight in the ceiling.

We were nearly completely undressed by the time the elevator reached upstairs. We had to start seeing more of each other as it was too far in between our sexual encounters.

We got through our first mad frenzy and then hit the shower. The second time was much slower and we spent more time enjoying the feel of each other. Damn this woman is gorgeous, but I blacked out after that second close encounter.

Chapter 18

. . . .

June 23 Sunday Morning

I woke up with the sun in my eyes. I could smell coffee brewing and also bacon cooking. That's enough to wake anyone up. Not only was she beautiful, but she can cook to.

I got up and went into the bathroom to drain the tiger and wash up. As I came out back into the bedroom Jane is walking in with a tray of food. The best part of it was that she forgot to get dressed. Life doesn't get any better than this. A gorgeous woman, a great-smelling breakfast and the morning sun shining in the doors. And it's all for me. Am I lucky or what? Oh, I forgot, she also had the Sunday paper tucked under her arm. I wonder if she had to go outside for the paper. Maybe someone else had a good morning too.

We had our breakfast and decided to have some dessert to finish it off. Dessert ended up being even better than the meal. Of course, dessert usually is better.

We spent the next couple of hours reading the Sunday paper. Of course, we did it in bed, which is very relaxing. It wasn't all relaxing, though. This woman must think I'm a machine. At noon I conceded that I needed a break. We decided to go to Barb's Diner for some lunch. I know it seems like all we do is eat. But we burned up a lot of calories working out. Who needs a gym? Not me!

After lunch I said goodbye to Jane. I said I would pick her up at six o'clock and we'd go out for a pizza. We have a great pizza parlor here in Black Crow.

It's Jim and Gina's Italian Pies. The owners, Jim and Gina Laguardi are actually from Italy. You can't beat their pizza and garlic bread.

I next stopped at the police station to see if the chief got the warrant to get Mr. Sagget's DNA test. When I arrived there, the chief wasn't in. But there was a message for me from the chief. He was letting me know that he got a warrant signed, but couldn't get ahold of Sagget's lawyer. He would keep trying and planned to interrogate Sagget in the morning.

I was still puzzled that we had no luck on anyone finding Jack Sampson. He had to have left the area, what with all the searching we have been doing. I had done some searching on the computer, but could find nothing on him. The small amount of papers we found in his house didn't tell us much. He had mostly bills and junk mail. There was nothing personal about him to be found. I think he must have another residence somewhere. I did a search for the whole state of Wisconsin for property taxes and deeds for any property he might own. I came up blank on everything. I also checked for anyone with the last name of Sampson. I thought maybe he grew up around here and maybe his folks had property.

I only found the name once. It was for a house right here in Black Crow. But they had been in their eighties when they passed away. There was a young family living in the house now. And there was nothing listed for them having any children.

I had my doubts about Jack Sampson being the killer. It was just a gut feeling I had. With all the illegal merchandise he had in the house, you would think some of the stolen jewelry would have been found there. He didn't seem bright enough to hide it somewhere else.

I decided to grab my fishing pole and head out to my fishing hole and do some thinking. So I ran by my house and grabbed my fishing pole and headed to my favorite spot. As I got near my fishing spot on Crabs Lake, I see something shiny through the brush.

It's pretty rough terrain and secluded around this side of the lake. You could almost get lost on the trails that run through the brush. You get in this area and the brush is tall and thick. You can't see any distance at all until you get to the water.

Anyways I head for the spot I saw the metal. I come around a curve in the trail and low and behold there's what looks like Sampson's Bronco. I stop quickly and stoop down in case he's around somewhere. I know he is armed and I'm sure probably dangerous.

I get on my cell phone and see I have a very weak signal. Being in northern Wisconsin there's not a lot of cell towers. So sometimes it's hard to get a signal. I dial 9-1-1 and get an answer. The dispatcher's voice is cutting in and out. I speak as loudly as I dare and give my location. I tell her to send backup but without sirens. I didn't want to spook Sampson if he's here and have him take off on me. I ask the dispatcher to repeat what I said before I hang up.

I stay by my car and try to hear any sounds Sampson might be making. All I get is total silence. So I decide to get closer and see if I can get a license number off the Bronco. I get close enough to see the rear license plate and make a mental note of it. I then crept back to my car and call it in.

Bingo, its Sampson's vehicle. I then hear a vehicle approaching behind me. It's Rob and he has another deputy with him. They pull up to me and exit their car. I inform them that it's Sampson's Bronco, and I haven't heard or seen any sign of him. I inform them to be careful because he probably still has a gun with him.

I then have Rob go around the left side and work his way towards the back of the Bronco. And I tell Steve, the deputy that came with Rob, to go around the right side. I tell them that I'll go straight in.

"Try to take him alive if you confront him, but don't take a chance of letting him shoot you. We each have a radio with us so put them on channel number fifty and turn the volume down. That's a channel that doesn't get used much. Rob, if you come upon Sampson key your mike twice and we'll come help you. Steve if you see him key yours three times so we'll know it's you. I'll key mine four times to alert both of you. Okay let's get going."

I pull my pistol out and head for the Bronco. I approach it slowly and come up on the back side. I see no one and cannot sense anything around the area. In the next minute, I see Rob and Steve coming to the front of the Bronco. We go up to the vehicle and look in the windows. It appears empty, so we try the doors. It's unlocked, so we quickly open the doors and find an empty vehicle. The keys are still in the ignition. I turn the key on and see there's plenty of gas in it according to the gas gauge.

"He must have ditched the vehicle here and has some place to hide not too far away. Let's spread out and see if we can find any tracks in the sand. It could give us an idea which way he headed. This area doesn't get used much so any tracks would probably be Sampson's."

We spread out and tracked a big circle around the Bronco. Steve called out. We went to where he called from and he pointed to the ground. There were footprints in the sand leading north towards the town of Chaney. We followed them for about a mile. They seemed to be headed straight to Chaney. I sent Steve back to get their squad car and meet us on the edge of Chaney.

Rob and I kept on going for about another half a mile and finally hit Suffolk Road, which goes into Chaney. It also runs east with a few farms out that way.

"My best guess would be that he probably went to Chaney. He would need to eat and sleep somewhere. I couldn't see him going east on Suffolk Road because there isn't much cover. But I figured we could check out the few farms that way just to be safe. That wouldn't take that long."

Steve saw us on the side of the road and picked us up. I told him to take us back to my car.

"I think we should start by checking out the two or three farms down Suffolk Road first. And then we can concentrate on the town of Chaney. You two can take the first farm and I'll start with the second one. If there's a third we'll check it together."

The farm I went to was pretty run-down. It had an old two-story farmhouse. I couldn't tell what color it should have been. Just about all the paint had peeled off over the years. There was an old barn still standing plus a few out buildings. None of them had any paint left on them either.

I knocked on the side door and waited. I heard footsteps coming to the door. It was an elderly woman that looked to be around eighty years old. I told her I was from the police department and asked if she had seen anyone around lately. She said the only person she had seen lately was her son. He came out about twice a week with groceries and to check up on her.

I asked if it was all right to check out the barn and out buildings. She said to go ahead but wasn't responsible if any of the buildings collapsed on me. I thanked her and did a quick search of the buildings. Upon not finding anyone, I headed out to the third farm.

Rob and Steve were already there and had searched the area. The farm was abandoned and starting to fall apart. The house wasn't safe to enter and the barn wasn't much better.

Rob said, "When we were at the first house, we talked to a young woman there. She and her husband actually farmed the area. They had about five hundred acres in crops. Most of it was up along Paddock Road on both sides. No one lived on Paddock Road for about five miles. There are various spots of woods up and down it. Paddock road was just around the corner from their farm."

"The woman said her husband had been up there cultivating corn on and off for the last week. He mentioned to her that he thought he saw some smoke coming from up the road in a big patch of woods. He said it was about twenty acres of woods, and he saw it more than once. It was a couple of miles up the road, so he didn't go check on it. She thought it was on the left side of the road. Her husband was gone today at a farm auction in Cambridge."

"Let's run over there and check it out. Hopefully, we can spot the right woods. I'm going to call it in just to be on the safe side. You never know what to expect out here. I remember back about six or seven years when a group of mercenaries moved into an old farm out south of Black Crow."

"When there was a lot shooting heard out there, the police department got tons of phone calls. I heard the chief sent a squad car out there to check it out. When they got there, they were stopped at the entrance into the farm by armed guards. They were denied entrance, so they called the chief. He went out there, and when he got there, they had barricaded the entrance with wagons loaded with bales of hay. When he got a bullhorn out and demanded to talk to someone, they started to shoot at him and the other officers."

"They ended up calling the state police and getting a SWAT team brought in. It took them a couple of days to get them out of there. They ended up with a couple of wounded officers in the end. Turns out there were only four guys holed up in there."

So we head over to Paddock Road. It runs to the north off of Suffolk Road. It starts out pretty open at first, and then I see some small wooded areas in the distance. Then about two miles up the road, I see a good-size woods on the left side of the road. I don't see any smoke as I approach the woods. Once there I see a dirt path going into the trees. It's a very thick wooded area, so you can't see very far into it. I stop and get out of the car to talk to Rob and Steve. I decide to go first and have them stay back a ways in case of any surprises.

I get back in my car and head down the dirt path. It's pretty tight with tree branches scraping the car as I go in. Up ahead I see a clearing coming up. I'm just about to the clearing when a shot rings out. It hits the upper part of my windshield leaving a hole with cracks leading off it.

I turn the car sharp to the left and stop quickly. I jump out so I'm blocked from the old barn I see in the clearing. I then grab the radio and call Rob and Steve to not come all the way up. I then call in to dispatch for some backup. I crawl into the car and grab the shotgun. The bullhorn is in the trunk, which I don't dare try to get at.

The next thing I know, Rob and Steve have snuck up to my car. I said we need a bullhorn so we can talk to whoever is shooting at us. Steve volunteers to go back and get the one from the other car.

When Steve gets back, I get the bullhorn. I turn it on and turn to talk to whoever is in the barn. I have a suspicion that it might be Sampson.

"Hello the barn. Who am I talking to? This is the Black Crow police department. Come out with your hands up without your weapon."

All of a sudden, it sounds like world war three. We start getting pelted with bullets coming from the barn. There's got to be three or four guns firing at us. All the glass is shot out of the car and I hear the tires whistling as the air escapes from them. All is quiet again.

"Stop your shooting. Who's in there and why are you shooting at us?"

I'll be damn if they didn't start shooting at us again. I don't know how much more this car will take. I reach up and fire a couple of shots at the barn along with Rob and Steve. Just as we duck back down, we get pelted by about a hundred shots again.

"We have to make a run for it back to the other car. With the amount of lead they're throwing at us this car isn't going to take much more. We'll regroup back there."

We took off one at a time without any more shots being fired. They were either reloading or getting low on ammo.

Just as we get to the other car two more police cars pull in. One is the chief with another officer with him. The other car has two more officers in it. I fill in the chief on what has happened and that the other car has more holes in it than swiss cheese.

"I figure there's at least three or four people in the barn. And they must have an arsenal in there with all the shooting they're doing. They won't even answer me when I try to talk to them. If I had to guess I think one of them might be Jack Sampson.

"Chief, I have an idea. We have seven of us here which I guess is about the whole of your department. We either have to call in the state to help us or try something else. I figure we split up and two go around one side and two the other way. Then the three that are left get as close as possible that's safe. The three in the front then open fire on the barn to give the other four a chance to flank the barn. Then the chief can use the bullhorn and call out to the barn and let them know they're surrounded. Hopefully they'll play it smart and surrender. Otherwise we'll rush them from the sides at the same time the three in front fire high to head them off. We can use our radios to coordinate the whole thing. We need to see what there are for doors on the sides and back. We can do that when we get back there. What do you think, chief?"

"I think it's worth a try. But if it looks too dangerous, then you need to pull back. If that happens, we'll call in the state's SWAT team. If anyone doesn't feel all right doing this, say so now. Also make sure you have enough ammo on you."

Everyone agreed to go for it.

Rob and I took off to the right side of the barn and two other officers went to the left. We swung far out circling around to the barn. When we were ready to head in toward the barn, I called the chief on the radio to open up on the barn.

They started shooting, and we started running to the barn. We reached the barn and the shooting stopped. I checked the back side of the barn to see if there was a back door. I didn't see one so I went back to the side by Rob. We had a door on our side. It was one of those old two-piece doors where the top is separate from the bottom. I checked with the guys on the other side to see if they had a door. They had no door, so I told them to sneak up towards the front of the barn and wait.

I tried the two-piece door and found the top unlocked and the bottom locked. I whispered to Rob that we would fling the top open when the shooting started and use the bottom as a shield. I then called the chief to start firing up high and we were going in.

The shooting started so Rob threw the top door open and we looked in. Three guys were looking out the front door with rifles in their hands. I hollered for them to drop their weapons, and I put a shot into the floor right behind them. Two of them swung their rifles up and started firing.

We ducked out of the way and tried to return fire without looking. I heard one scream out. Apparently, we hit one. Then all shooting stopped at once. I called into the barn telling them to drop their weapons and put their hands up. I got no answer, so I snuck a peek first towards the back of the barn and then the front.

There was some old machinery and an enclosed box truck in there plus some bales of hay stacked here and there. I caught a glimpse of someone behind some bales. All of a sudden, a gun appeared and he started firing. I ducked, but Rob caught a stray shot and went down. I quickly checked him out and luckily it just nicked his shoulder. I heard the two officers from the front go in the front door and some shots fired. They radioed that they had one of their shooters down. Luckily Rob wasn't too bad off. He had a clean handkerchief on him so I slid it under his shirt and pressed it to his wound. I told him to keep pressure on it.

I then heard some noisy racket coming from the back of the barn. I ran back there and as I turned the corner, I ran right into someone. One of the shooters was breaking out. He crashed into me as he broke through the wood and we both went falling to the ground.

It was Jack Sampson. He reached for his gun that he dropped when he ran into me. I managed to kick it away, but then he was jumping on top of me. He started throwing punches at my face. I heard and felt my nose snap, which really pissed me off.

With all the fights I'd been in over the years, I'd never broken my nose. He was straddling me so I brought my knee up into his baby maker. That stopped the punches right away. I pushed him off and came down on him with my knee into his chest. I then accidently hit across his face with my fist and heard his nose snap. And then when I brought my fist back across his face the other way, I heard it snap again. I did apologize as I told him he was under arrest. I rolled him over and pinned his arms behind him and slipped the cuffs on him. He was cussing and swearing up a storm. He screamed that he was going to sue me for using excessive force. I told him to shut the hell up or I'd give him a reason to bitch.

I got him up and went around the barn to see how Rob was doing. Rob had a handkerchief pressed on his wound. He said he was fine, and it was just a scratch. I checked with the chief on the radio and told him we had everything under control. I said we also needed the EMTs out here for Rob and the prisoners.

I pushed Sampson and he fell to the ground. I got him back up and shoved him around the barn towards the front. When we got there, I saw that the other two officers had the third shooter in handcuffs and apparently the shooter that got hit was dead. I double-checked and could find no pulse. He had been hit twice, once in the leg and the other looked like it went right to the heart. Apparently, the other shooter had given up as soon as his buddy got hit.

The chief said the coroner and EMT's were on their way. He also sent two officers to try and clear the drive so they could get in. He also called for a tow truck to move the shot-up police car. We then walked the prisoners out to the squad cars and put them in the back seats.

The chief and I then went back to the barn to check it out. The truck parked in there was a twenty-foot straight truck. The doors were unlocked so we opened them. It was completely full of brand-new computers and television sets. There were desktop and laptop computers. And we could also see a whole pallet of iPads. This load had to be worth at least two or three hundred thousand dollars. It was stacked tight to the roof of the truck.

We looked around and saw a ladder that went up to a loft on one end of the barn. We climbed the ladder and found another load of the same thing as in the truck. This had to come from some warehouse somewhere. I told the chief that we had better get the state boys in on this. It's a little too big for us. He agreed and went to put a call into them.

Once the coroner got there, we took off. We left the two officers, Dan and Joey to hold down the fort. The chief took one car with one prisoner and I took the other. I took Rob with me to drop him at the hospital.

I took Rob there and we went in with Sampson to have his nose fixed up. While there they also looked at my nose. They said there wasn't much they could do for mine. They suggested I go see an ENT doc for a second opinion.

I then took Rob and Sampson back to the police station. Once there the chief told Rob to go home for the rest of the day. Rob didn't want to go, but the chief ordered him to go.

Then I supposed I'd have to write up this report. Rob has been doing our reports, but with his wound, I supposed I could do it. That's one of the reasons I quit the police force. I hate sitting at a desk filling out papers. Life is too short for that, but there is a reason for it.

I found an empty desk that looked comfortable enough. It had a computer at it so I fired it up. The department was up to date enough to have the basic forms loaded in the computers, so that would save some time. So I dug into it, hoping my typing skills weren't too rusty.

I got to thinking how we now had two people in custody that could be suspects in the murders. I didn't really like Sagget for all the murders. I think he tried to make it look the same as the other murders, but didn't know all the facts of the others. Hopefully the lab could identify the blood on a knife as coming from his wife. That wouldn't prove that she was stabbed with it. They could say she cut herself while using it to prepare food. But it would help as circumstantial evidence against John Sagget as the murderer. I also think we can break him upon interrogation. Or at least get a confession with the promise of a lesser charge.

I also don't think Jack Sampson is the murderer. It would be nice to have him be the one, but there is absolutely no evidence tying him to it. I do think he's definitely guilty of major theft. We'll probably end up handing him over to the state police for that. We have the merchandise, but they can find out where it came from and it could possibly be an interstate theft, which would be the FBI's territory.

I spend the next hour getting the arrest reports typed up. Then the chief calls me to his office. I get in there and he informs me that we will interrogate Sampson tomorrow morning. His lawyer is coming from out of town, and he won't talk to us without him.

He says, "I hope to have the lab results Monday morning on Betty Sagget so we can interrogate him. I personally think he only killed his wife. What we know and have for evidence seems to point that way. So, Duke go ahead and take the rest of the day off and we'll see you early tomorrow."

So I take off, and I'm thinking a nice dinner and maybe dessert with Jane. I have her on speed dial, so I punch it in. She answers after about ten rings and sounds all out of breath. I jokingly asked if I was interrupting anything. She knew what I was referring to and said he just left. There's nothing like sticking my foot in my mouth. She then told me that it was much better than the other guy she very seldom sees.

So I said, "Since I'm your third lover, I thought maybe you'd like to go for dinner tonight. I'm sure I can show you a much better time than those other two. They probably make you go Dutch when going out on a date."

"Well, Mr. Smooth talker, I'd guess I need to eat and as long as you're buying, how can I refuse. But it's strictly a plutonic date. I'm pretty worn out already so I need my rest. Maybe if you're nice I'll let you give me a good-night kiss. What time will you and your chariot arrive?"

"I'll pick you up at seven o'clock. How does a nice big juicy steak from the Chuck Wagon Inn sound? I'll even spring for lobster if you want it."

"You had better have the steak yourself. You're going to need the protein before the night is over. You will need all the energy you can dig up if you think you can catch me."

Well, we got our meal in and she was right about my needing the extra protein. I staggered home around midnight feeling like a whipped pup. I needed to get some sleep because tomorrow was going to be a long day. What with two interrogations to get through. Hopefully we could get some cases solved.

Chapter 19

. . . .

June 24 Monday

I woke up at six thirty feeling like I had a hangover. I don't think I could keep up with Jane if we were living together. Maybe I need to start working out to get my stamina built up. She is one fantastic woman.

Anyways I got my shower in and headed to Barb's for some coffee and breakfast. The diner was busy and seemed to be getting its business back. I think word got out that we made a couple of arrests so people probably think we have the killer. I hope they're right, but I have several doubts.

I got my breakfast in without too many questions asked. I even drank extra coffee to get all the bugs out of my brain. I needed to be clearheaded for the interviews. Then I headed to the station to get the day started.

I walked into the station and was met by the chief. He said they were bringing Sampson into the interrogation room now. We headed for the room to wait for him. He was brought in handcuffed and also with leg cuffs. We got Sampson seated and had him sign a form stating that he understood his rights.

Rob had a small recorder to get everything on record. He tested it to make sure it was working and recorded Jack Sampson's full name and the date of this session. He also added our names as being present as witnesses. The chief had already told me to start the interrogation and if he thought of anything else, he would inject it.

"Mr. Sampson, or can I call you Jack to simplify things?"

Sampson replied, "I really don't give a shit what you call me. I'm not answering any of your questions anyways. I was just hanging around that barn having a few beers. I should sue your ass for false arrest and police brutality."

"Well, Jack, maybe you forgot about shooting at us the other night and running away. Plus, yesterday when you were shooting at us again. Plus, we have you for attempted murder of a police officer. You wounded Detective Rob Turner, who happens to be the police chief's brother. And you led us on a pretty rough chase after the first shooting. When we checked out your house after that, we found it had a ton of stolen merchandise in it. Those two things alone will get you a nice long prison sentence. You also shot up a squad car; we'll probably have to total it with all the holes in it. You're also a prime suspect in two murder cases."

"Murder, are you kidding me! I haven't killed anyone. I might be a thief, but I don't do killing. Your way off base there."

"What do you call shooting at us as many times as you did? You didn't seem to be shooting over our heads. We have a squad car full of bullet holes from you to prove it."

"I meant that I didn't have a thing to do with killing those two couples. That's completely sick, cutting people up like that. I don't have the stomach for something like that."

"Well, that can be cleared up if you have alibis for two Saturdays in a row. The dates are the evenings of June 8 and June 17. If you have a good alibi for those two nights, then that will clear you on the four murder charges."

"How the hell do you expect me to remember that long ago? Let me see a calendar so I can get it straight in my head."

Rob went out and grabbed a calendar and brought it in. He handed it to Sampson.

"Well, the first Saturday I was at the Dugout Bar in Chaney. I remember that I went to see the blues band they had playing that night. I spent all night there right up to closing. You can ask Rocky the owner because I sat at the bar all night. He waited on me most of the time."

"The next Saturday I was down by Madison on business. I never made it back here until the next day."

"So what were you doing down there all night that would have to do with business? You don't appear to be that much of a business man."

"It was private business that is none of your business. And I do have a witness to prove I was there."

"What are the names of your witnesses? I'll call them and get this all cleared up right now."

"I was actually with the two men that were in the barn yesterday with me."

"Well, one of them is dead, and we have yet to talk to the other one. I'm sure if you were with those two, that it probably was something illegal. I'm sure when we sweat your buddy that he'll give up what you guys were up to. So whoever talks first is going to get any deal we can give you."

"What kind of deal are we talking about?"

"It will help you out at your sentencing for shooting at us, which is attempted murder of law enforcement officers. I see you going away for the majority of the rest of your miserable life."

"Okay, okay, we were down in Fitchberg at a Best Buy warehouse loading our truck with electronics. Johny has a buddy that works there, and he set up the heists both times. It took us until midnight to finish, and then we were too tired to drive back. So we found a roach motel to stay in for the night that was about ten miles away. While there, we worked on a case of beer, that Snake had bought, and then we crashed for the night. That's the truth, and I have never killed anyone. I've done a lot of bad things in my life, but killing is not my style. And I really doubt that I was the one to shoot officer Turner because I'm a lousy shot. Most of my shots were in the air above you. Like I said I don't get into shooting people. And I'm sorry that you got shot officer. We were just trying to scare you all off."

"Well, Jack, we're going to check all this out. Here's a pad of paper and a pen. We want you to write all this down just the way it happened. You were lucky you didn't seriously hurt Rob here or it would be much worse. You're also lucky Officer Turner is such a good-natured person or we'd let him spend some private time in this room with you."

The chief and I left Rob with Sampson and headed to his office. He wanted to talk about what we just heard and where I thought we stood on our cases now.

"What do you think, Duke? It doesn't appear that Sampson is our killer. If his alibis hold up, that will seriously eliminate him. That only leaves us with John Sagget. What are your thoughts on him?"

"I don't think Sampson did it either. We definitely have enough to put him away for a long time. I also think Sagget killed his wife. Everything points to him. But I don't like him for the other two murders. There wasn't any glass broken in a door. And the electricity wasn't turned off in the house. It's also weird that only the wife was killed but not him. He also isn't acting innocent. I've never seen anyone so nervous before. An innocent person acts nervous, but not that bad. Plus, he ran which really makes him look guilty. The coroner couldn't tell if the killer was left or right-handed in the Sagget murder. There was only one stab wound. Sagget is right-handed also. As shook up as he's been, I don't see him having the balls to do the other killings."

"What time is Sagget's lawyer coming in, chief? Do you want me in on that session? I realize we need to proceed carefully so as not to have him going to the hospital again."

"Yes, I think you should handle that interrogation to. You handle things very well and have more experience than any of us. His lawyer said he'd be here at about ten o'clock this morning. You definitely got Sampson to talk quickly. He didn't even ask for a lawyer."

"I also wanted to apologize to you for my youngest son's treatment of you. I've had to bring Rick up pretty much by myself since my wife passed away. I'm afraid I didn't really know what I was doing. And I was too soft on him. My wife Sofie, God rest her soul, was the main parent in raising the other children. She knew what she was doing. That's the main reason his brother Rob, is such a good kid. She spent time with him and taught him well."

"I'm still hoping that Rick will come around. If he doesn't, I don't know where he'll end up."

"I'm sorry about your wife chief, and I hope Rick comes around. Maybe he needs to go off to school or get a job. He just needs some responsibility to give him a reason to feel wanted. I will definitely act differently if he confronts me again. I'll try to be more tactful and reason with him."

"I'm going to go write up my report now while it's still fresh in my mind. Plus, it will help kill time before Sagget's lawyer shows up. I hope we can get a break on the two murders. But I don't know where it will come from yet. I think we need to do more history on the victims. There has to be a connection somehow between them."

Sagget's lawyer showed up right at ten o'clock. The chief and I both met him and introduced ourselves. He introduced himself as Steven Kilroy. He came up from Madison. The chief called back to have Sagget brought up to the interrogation room. We then proceeded to the interrogation room to wait for him.

Once we were all settled in, the chief reminds John Sagget that he has been read his rights. He says he has and the chief has him sign the form that he acknowledged it. Then his lawyer asks what the charges are against his client.

The chief opens up the folder he brought with him and reads out loud. "First charge is two counts of shooting at police officers, which is attempted murder of police officers. The second charge is arson. And the third charge is the murder of his wife. There's also a charge of fleeing police after shooting at them. We didn't charge for fleeing the police from the hospital because he was only wanted for questioning at that time."

Mr. Kilroy then asks to have some time to confer with Mr. Sagget about all the charges. The chief agrees so the chief, Rob, and myself all leave the room.

It got to be twelve o'clock, and my stomach is growling. I asked the chief about leaving for a quick bite to eat. He said to go ahead and bring him a sandwich back. If Sagget and his lawyer got finished before I returned, he would have them take a lunch break.

I got back to the station at about one thirty. Everyone was ready to start. I handed the chief his sandwich and went to wait in the interrogation room. Shortly after, everyone came in. Rob got the recorder fired up, and I started by asking Sagget if he was feeling all right. He said he was fine and to get the show on the road.

I asked, "Why did you run after we took you to the hospital? We had only brought you in to ask some questions."

"I don't know why you couldn't ask me the questions at the motel. I figured you were going to pin the murder of my wife on me. I loved my wife and would never hurt her. I see enough on TV to know the spouse is the first suspect."

"Well, who do you suspect could be responsible for your wife's death?"

"It was probably the same person that killed those other folks. It stands to reason that someone is killing older retired folks around here."

"Well, the other killings have facts attributed to them that were not disclosed to the public. Your wives murder is in no way similar. Also, from talking to you it appears there's no love lost between the two of you. You speak pretty negatively about her. Plus, the neighbors have heard you talking down to her repeatedly. And we have the murder weapon. You even admitted to us that you didn't expect her to live this long. Plus, it's a hell of a coincidence that your wife's murder is done right after the other murders. And it's also odd that only your wife was killed and not you. Doesn't that seem odd that the murderer would leave you alive?"

"The way I see it we definitely have you for evading police, shooting at police, which is attempted murder. And we also have you for arson, trying to burn your own house down. You're also on the suspects list for the other two killings around here."

"If you want any consideration on these charges, we need your admission for killing your wife and the other two couples. We will eventually figure it out, and then you'll get the maximum sentence. Your admission will only help you by saving us extra work. It's your call. It could mean the difference between manslaughter and first-degree murder. We'll leave you with your lawyer to discuss it."

We all left the room and headed for the coffee machine. I noticed there was a donut left from this morning, so I grabbed it. For some reason I had a sugar craving.

The chief asked how I thought it went in there.

I told him, "I think if he's smart, he'll pony up and admit to the killing. He knows that we're going to have enough to convict him. At least his lawyer should realize that. But I don't see him being our killer of the two couples. I don't think he's that smart, plus he would have copied all the facts we found of the other murders."

After about twenty minutes Mr. Kilroy comes out and says they're ready to talk. So we all head in and get the recorder going.

Mr. Kilroy starts, "We need to know what kind of deal you're offering here."

The chief says, "I can't make any promises without talking to the district attorney first. But I would say if Mr. Sagget admits to all the murders, we could take off the charges for the shooting and arson. Let me call the DA and get him in here."

The chief makes the call and about five minutes later the DA shows up. His name is George Popem. Yes, that's his real name. He even uses it for advertising at election time. He advertises that "the police catch 'em and I'll pop 'em."

Once everyone is introduced and we bring George up to date, he agrees with what the chief told them. And we would need it all in writing.

Mr. Kilroy says, "Mr. Sagget is admitting to the killing of his wife, but had nothing to do with those other murders. He didn't even know those other people and was at home with his wife on those nights. He admits to only the one killing."

"Here's what we're going to do. I'll drop the charges on the shooting and the arson. We'll charge Mr. Sagget with second degree murder for his wife. If we later find he had anything to do with the other murders, we will prosecute to the full extent of the law. If you agree to this, then take this pad and write it all out in your own words."

So Rob, the chief, and I left the room and went to the chief's office. We did, of course, leave a deputy outside the door to guard the prisoner.

The chief says, "That was good work, Duke. We've solved two cases today, and it's only Monday. So, Duke, do you have and new ideas on how to proceed on the other killings? We really have to get it figured out. I've got the mayor and city council on my back to get it done."

"Since Rob is on limited duty from his wound, I think we'll hit the computer and phones to do some deep research. We have to dig into the victims' backgrounds and see what pops up. The killer has to have some connection to the two couples somehow."

Rob and I went to our desks. I told Rob, "Why don't you see what can be found on the computer for any history on the Andersons and Browning's. See what their work history was for, say, the last thirty years. I suppose we should also check out the kids' histories also. See what jobs they've had and if they got into any trouble. I'm going to check out their houses again to see if we missed anything. I'm also going to check back with the neighbors to see if anything new pops up. I'll see you later."

I spent an hour at each house and found nothing new. I then had an idea. I called Rob to see if he found anything. He told me he was still working on it and would see me in the morning.

I suggested he meet me at my house. I wanted him to help me check out my basement if he felt up to it. He told me he felt fine. Just a little sore, but ibuprofen helped a lot. I told him to have a good evening, and I'd see him in the morning.

Chapter 20

. . . .

June 25 Tuesday

I got up at seven o'clock and hit the shower right away. I then got the coffee pot going so it would be ready when Rob arrived. At quarter to eight there was a knock at the door. It was Rob, and he had a pretty good-sized folder with him. I see he also had a box of donuts from the Cunningham bakery.

I poured us some coffee, and when I opened the box of donuts, I told Rob I was in love. There's nothing better in the morning than a good cup of coffee and frosted donuts. I love frosted donuts as long as there's no sprinkles on them. I'm glad I have an active metabolism and can keep the weight off. Otherwise I'd be as big as a house. I wonder if Jane would still have me then.

I said to have a seat and we'd go over his findings while having our coffee and donuts. Rob got his papers out and started with the Andersons.

"George Anderson worked at the Black Crow Bank until 1983. He was the bank president for the last ten years he worked there. He then left to work in Chicago as an investment counselor. He started his own investment firm called Anderson Investments. His wife's name was Anna and she was a home-maker. They never had any children, at least none that I could find."

"Ed and Carol Browning have been here for about eight years this time around. He was and insurance agent for American Liberty Insurance for thirty-five years. He retired ten years ago. Liberty Insurance covered mostly house and car insurance. They also did some life insurance business."

"The Browning's did live here in the late sixties, and early seventies. That was when he started selling insurance. His wife, Carol, was a homemaker also. They had two children, a son and a daughter. The son's name is John Browning and daughter is Diane Ames."

"The Andersons had hundred-thousand-dollar life insurance policies on each other. The money is to go to various charities. Mostly kids' charities such as St. Jude's and Shriners Hospital. Some goes to their church also. The same goes with all their other holdings. I couldn't come up with how much that was without a court order. But in their wills, it all goes to charity."

"The Browning's had fifty-thousand-dollar life insurance on each of them. Their wills left everything to be divided evenly to their kids. The same with the rest of their estate which is mainly the house and a few stocks."

"I couldn't find any criminal records for any of them. The parents and kids were all clean and have no records at all. The only connection I see so far is that they all lived around here back in the sixties and seventies. And then they all moved back here in the recent past."

"Well, Rob, that is interesting. I wonder if it has something to do with when they all lived here years ago. Both men were in lines of work that come in contact with the public. Insurance and banking both have to do with money. You borrow money at a bank for a car and home and then need to insure both. But I'll be damned if I see a link to their deaths. It gives some more to think about."

"Rob, do you feel up to a trip to my basement to see what we may see?"

"Sounds good to me. What exactly happened here on those nights?"

"Well, on the first night, the night the Andersons were killed, I was awoken by the sound of breaking glass. My electricity seemed to be off. So I got up and grabbed the old baseball bat I keep under the bed and my flashlight. I snuck downstairs to the kitchen and didn't hear anything. I turned on the flashlight and saw glass broken out of the door. It was weird because there was no glass on the kitchen floor. It had been broken from the inside out. All the broken glass was out on the porch floor."

"I then went to the basement to have a look and get the electricity back on. When I got the juice back on, I checked the basement out. There was no one there, and I didn't notice anything out of place."

"The night of the second killing I had been out with you hanging out at all the bars to see what we could hear. I got home around one thirty to find my house all dark. I went to the back door and stepped on glass outside the door. I went in and went right to the basement to get the electricity back on. Once I got it back on, I checked the whole house out and found nothing out of place or missing. Whatever was going on it seemed to originate in the basement. So I figured we would start down there."

We headed downstairs with a couple of flashlights to check out dark areas. I told Rob that I wanted to get the house rewired. So, while we were down here, I was going to see what type of old wiring was used. Maybe get an idea of what needed to be redone.

We split up and each took half the basement. We looked in every nook and cranny for anything that seemed odd. We got done and all we found was a lot of dirt and cobwebs. It just didn't make any sense.

I got looking then at the ceiling and found that most of the wiring was the old knob and tube wiring. This was the old white flaky wiring that ran through porcelain insulators. A lot of fires had started from old wiring such as this. So it looked like it all needed to be replaced.

I did notice some metal electrical boxes that had been added through the years. Off of some there was Romex wire running up into the walls. Probably for outlets that had been added over the years. Romex is the newest type of wire on the market now. It had a durable plastic covering on it. I also saw some metal shielded cable ran in a couple of spots.

I'm no electrician, but this wiring did not look safe. I walked around the perimeter of the basement tracking the wiring. I could account for all the wires going up to outlets. I got to the east side of the house and found a weird thing. I called Rob over and told him to take a look.

A wire ran along high up in the floor joist and came to a metal electric box. It had all been painted with flat black paint, which made it hard to see. In fact, you would never see it without a flashlight. There was a wire running over to one of the basement lights. Then there was another wire running off the back side into the wall. Most of the Romex wire that I've seen has always been white. This one was painted flat black to try and hide it. I didn't know if it was painted maybe because it wasn't up to the electrical code.

That side of the basement had a wooden wall built and anchored in place. Then it was covered with plywood and painted flat black. Wood shelving was then put up and anchored to the wall. The shelves had different odd boxes and old junk sitting on it.

Anyways I told Rob," look here, the wire looks like it goes right through the outside portion of the floor joist above the wood shelving. Let's go upstairs and see if there's an outlet there."

We went up to the living room, which is on the east side of the house. We checked the wall out and found two outlets on the wall, but they were closer to the room corners. Plus, I could account for those two lines off boxes in the basement. The wire we saw downstairs would have come up in the center of the wall. So we decided to go outside and see if maybe there was as outside outlet.

We got outside and checked all along the east wall. There was nothing there.

"Rob, it might have nothing to do with this, but if you look, you'll notice the dead grass here. It's been like this since I bought this place. I've added grass seed and watered it and still the grass doesn't want to grow in this square. And why there would be an electric wire running to here is making no sense. Let's go back down to the basement and check that wall out."

Back in the basement we went over to the east wall. We started to take the boxes and such off the shelves. Then I started pulling on the shelving trying to break it loose from the wall. All of a sudden, the center section started to pull out. I slid it completely out and shoved it to the side. I had Rob shine his light on the wall to make it easier to see. There was a hole in the plywood wall about two inches round. I put my finger in the hole and pulled. That section of the wall started to swing open like a door.

I got it open all the way and Rob and I shined our flashlights where the wall had been. I said to Rob, "What the hell have we got here? I think we'd better call the chief. This might answer some questions, but still leave plenty more. So Rob, don't touch anything yet. We need to get the chief over here to see this first. It's also going to have to be examined for prints. Plus, I don't want us to be responsible for all of this."

I get my phone out and call the chief. "I think you might want to come over to my house to see something. I don't want to say too much over the phone. When you come don't use your siren or lights. I think we need to keep this under wraps for a while. If someone asks where you're going, just say you are going to join us for breakfast. Rob is here with me and we'll see you soon."

Ten minutes later the chief arrives. He comes to the back door where Rob and I are waiting for him. I invite him to come in to the basement.

"Chief, I had two break-ins into my house on the same nights as the two murders. The first one I didn't report because nothing seemed to be taken. Plus, I didn't know about the murders at the time. I did report the second one when the Browning's were killed. Rob and I decided to have a closer look at my place."

"We started in the basement and didn't find anything on a sweep of the area. I then decided to take a look at my house wiring, because I plan to have it rewired. While checking it out I found old and fairly new wiring. Then we found some that had been spray painted flat black. It's a branch coming off a junction box. It's Romex wire that's usually white in color. In checking we could not find what the wire goes to."

"So, we decided to move some of the shelving underneath it. We then found a plywood door which looked like the rest of the wall. But it had a hole in the middle on one side. When I put a finger in and pulled part of the wall opened up. It had hinges mounted on it. We just took a look without touching anything. I wanted you here as a witness."

We arrived at the east wall in the basement and turned on our flashlights. The chief let out a gasp when he looked in. I saw a light switch on the wall inside so I reached out and turned it on.

The chief says, "Oh my God, this is impossible. I wouldn't have believed you if you didn't show me this. This is unbelievable. It probably solves one piece of our robbery murders. We need a crime investigation crew in here to check for prints."

"Chief, I think we need to keep this quiet for a while. We need to catch whoever put this all in here."

"Obviously, they are also responsible for that body lying over there."

I did a double take at where the chief was pointing. I said, "What makes you say it's a body? All I see is a tarp covering something."

"Because doesn't that look like a shoe sticking out the end of it. Have you got some gloves we can use to check it out?"

Rob says to hold on and he runs up to his car and gets some.

We're sitting here looking at a room off the basement's east wall. It's about ten foot by ten foot. That explains why the grass doesn't grow worth a damn on the east side. There's not that much soil on top of this room. The room was probably built when the house was put up. It was probably built as a root cellar.

Rob returns and hand us all a pair of latex gloves. We glove up and walk into the room. I go over and lift a corner of the tarp and sure enough there's a body under it.

There's shelving about a foot deep on three walls. There are some canning jars strewn about. Most look empty, but some have jewelry shoved into them. Then there is a small table in the center of the room. On the table are piles of money. Most of it is bundled in money wraps. They're marked as one thousand dollars in each. There's also some lose money in bills and coins. We didn't want to touch any of it yet, until it could be checked for prints. But there had to be many thousands of dollars here. I guessed there to be over a hundred thousand dollars.

There are also two hunting-style knives lying on the table. They look clean but need to be checked out for any blood residue that could be left on them. Also, they need to be checked for fingerprints.

The worst part of it all was the skeleton lying in the corner. It was completely decomposed that we could see. It did have clothes, but they were rotting away. The clothing consisted of bib overalls and a plaid flannel shirt. It also had old-looking work boots on it.

The skull was shattered on the back side. It looked like cause of death was probably caused by a blow to the head.

My break-ins happened on the same nights as the theft and murders. But they seemed to happen shortly after. So, it seemed obvious that this jewelry and cash was probably from those crimes.

"Chief, the problem I see is if we have a crime scene crew come in everyone will know something odd is going on here. The killer will also hear of it and figure we found his stash. Then it takes away this opportunity to catch him when he comes back. I know we have a body here, but it has been for many years by the looks of it. I don't think waiting a while longer will make that much difference to him. Plus, it gives us a chance to catch the killer. We have a chance to solve three crimes here."

"I see your thinking, Duke. I guess it's not going to hurt anything to wait for a while. What can we do, though, to catch the perp? We can't stake out your house twenty-four hours a day. We don't have the personnel to do that. And a stakeout would be seen by all the neighbors. It's not like the big city where it's not unusual to have strange cars sitting around. I'm open to any suggestions from either one of you. Also, wouldn't the smell from that body have been pretty bad when it was rotting?"

"Yes, it would have been really bad. But if you look closely it looks like there was a white powder over and under the corpse. I would guess that's it's lime. There's a bunch of empty bags in the corner there. Most of it has dissolved with time. They probably covered it with the stuff pretty heavily to mask the smell. Farmers use lime a lot when burying livestock to keep predators from digging them up. It was also a staple in the old outhouses. When you had a bowel movement you would sprinkle some in the hole to hold the smell down."

"Plus, the door seems to seal fairly tight on the room here. I think we need to do a history check on this house and check out all the people that lived here. Rob, can you handle that? You should probably go back at least forty years by the look of the corpse. We'll need to know the owners and all their offspring. Probably should list any other relatives they also had. I'm sure some are still living in the area."

"The other thing I think we could do is set up some cameras to get a picture of the person coming down into my basement. One or two cameras put in the right spots could possibly get us a picture of our perp. They have these new infrared cameras that don't need a flash to take a picture. I don't know what something like that would cost. We need someone that knows electronics and can be trusted."

"You know, Duke, that's a great idea. I can have my son Rick, check it out. He's big in all the newest electronics. And I'll vouch for him or else I'll royally kick his ass. We can have him come over in civilian clothes like he's just visiting you. I'll have patrol cars run by here more often until we get something going. What do you think of Rob doing some fingerprinting in here? We also need an inventory of all this. But there should be at least two people doing it so we have a witness. He's pretty good at checking for fingerprints if his arm is okay. That could be done on the sly also. Maybe have him over for a cookout or something that seems normal."

"I think that's a good idea chief. Does your arm seem all right to you, Rob? If not, we can wait a day or two so it has more time to heal."

"No, Duke, my arm doesn't hurt at all. It was just a nick, which is no worse than a scratch. Plus, I'm anxious to see what we can find. I can start anytime you want."

Duke replies, "Also, Chief, why don't you just tell Rick that the camera is for the back door. We can just say that someone keeps breaking the glass in the door. It's not that I don't trust Rick, but I think we should keep what's in the basement to ourselves. The less that people know about it the better."

"Also, Rob, why don't you go back to the station and start checking out any the history of this house you can find on our computers. I'm going to go the courthouse to check records on recorded deeds and such. I might also hit the library and see what I can find there. They might have some records on file plus they should have all the old local newspapers on file. I'm hoping most of the old newspapers have been converted to the computer. But I really doubt it."

"Rob, why don't we figure on you coming over in the morning to start inventorying what's in the hidden basement room. If anyone asks why you're here, we'll say that we're brainstorming over coffee and donuts. We are cops so we need our donuts."

The Chief replies, "Well, guys, I think we have a plan here. So let's go and get started. I'm keeping my fingers crossed that this all works. Good luck."

I headed for the courthouse while Rob went back to the station. The courthouse is one of the oldest buildings in Black Crow. It's in the center of the town square. It was built in the late 1800s. And it's still an elegant-looking building with four huge white pillars across the front. The town has kept it up pretty well throughout the years.

It holds all the records for all of Monroe County. It is considered the county courthouse, even though it's not in the county seat. We only have one judge, and he handles mostly traffic violation cases. But he is capable of handling murder cases as well. His name is the Honorable Judge Jerry Hammond. You don't see many murder cases in these parts. Most of them that do happen are usually from domestic disputes that have gone to the extreme.

I believe many of the locals and others that have lived here for a long time, all probably own guns. Hunting is a popular pastime up here in God's country. I even own a few guns, but don't hunt anymore. They were handed down from my father to me. Besides I've seen enough killing to last me a lifetime.

My father, Mike Moran, loved northern Wisconsin. He was born and raised about fifty miles from here in the town of Sparta. They actually hunted for a lot of their food during the Great Depression. There was always plenty of deer, rabbits, and squirrels to hunt for. And they had a huge garden for vegetables. So they had it better than a lot other folks.

I head into the courthouse and go the second floor. Of course, a building as old as this has no elevator so I climb the old concrete steps. They're worn so much from all these years that you can feel the concave shape where thousands of people have stepped. I head on into the Register of Deeds office. I say hello to our register of deeds Markum Dooley. We get our hellos out of the way and I ask about seeing the deeds on my house going back to when it was built. He asks if there's a problem about the ownership. I tell him no, and I'm just curious about all the previous owners. I also wanted to see if any of the previous owners were still around in case I had any questions about the place. I explained that I was in the middle of remodeling it.

Markum excuses himself to go get the book we need. He explains that his department is just starting to transcribe the old records to computer. He returns with the book, which is huge. It's about two and a half feet wide and two foot high. He tells me it is the official Land Registry Title Deeds book.

I have to fill out a small form giving my name, address and date of birth. Markum says it's just for his records and it makes the transaction legal.

He flips through the book and finds my address. He then turns the book around so I can read it. Markum slides a piece of paper and pen over to me so I can write down the information. As I write I think I recognize one name. At least I think I do. The name Dick Jones sounds familiar. There are a lot of people named Jones out there, so I could be wrong. I'm thinking that might be JJ's grandfather. My list is fairly short, so it should be easier to check out.

1923—built by Burt Hines
1939—bought by Richard Jones
1972—bought by James Johnson
1990—bought by Duke Moran

Markus looks at the list with me and says he thinks that James Johnson might still live around here. He says the name seems to ring a bell to him.

I ask Markum how I can find out if these were just one person selling to another or if there could be other reasons they were sold. Such as probate, from a death or maybe from foreclosure on the property.

"I have no way of checking on that here, Duke. You could check the death records, which I think they keep track of in the clerk of courts office. They would also have records of any foreclosures that were done.

I thank Markum and head to the clerk of courts office, which is downstairs. I enter the clerk of courts office and find an old familiar face sitting there. Its

Judy Bush from my high school days. I say hello and we reminisce for about ten minutes. Judy and I dated a few times while in our sophomore year at good old Black Crow high school. She was always a very cute girl. She was and still is a sweet petite girl with some very nice curves. Even after having two children she has kept her small frame and youth. If she wasn't married, I'd probably ask her out now. Most of our problems years ago were mine. I just didn't want to be tied down to one girl back then. So we didn't really mesh too good, but did manage to stay good friends over the years.

Judy says, "I know you didn't just come in here to see me. What can I do for, Duke?"

"Well, Judy, it's always nice to see you, but I do have other reasons for being here. I'm looking for some information on my house. I'm trying to track down the past owners of my house and if they might still be around. I have some dates of the house being sold and Markum in the register of deeds thought I might get some information here. Such as possible repossessions, or if they went through probate court."

"Yes, we can check most of that in the computer. We have been gradually putting everything in the computer over the last two years. Why don't we start with the first sale on your list?"

"That would be a guy named Burt Hines. He was the first owner when it was built in 1923."

"Okay, I'll check the obituaries for 1922 and 1923 to first to see if he might have passed away. Okay, here we go, Burt Hines pasted away on August 20, 1938. You show that the house was closed on February 10, 1939. I'll check the court records for probate transactions after Mr. Hines's passing."

This took a little longer, but she did find it. "Here it is. It was probated on December 5, 1938. It shows the property was passed on to a John Hines, whom it says was his son. My guess would be that son John probably cleaned the house out and then put it up for sale."

"That appears to be what happened. Let me write that all down so I don't forget it. Can we see who purchased the house from son John?"

"Yes, we'll look in the transfer of deeds section. Here it is. The house was purchased by Richard Jones in February of 1939. Next transaction shown is the house being bought by a Jim Johnson in July of 1972. Let me check to see if Richard Jones is still alive."

"I can't find any records on Richard Jones. So he had to be alive when the house was bought by Jim Johnson. But going back to the deed transaction, I see that the house was sold by the Black Crow Bank. That means the bank somehow got possession on the property." Let me look in the foreclosure section in the computer. Ah-ha, here it is. The property was foreclosed on in 1971. So that explains how the bank got the property. And it looks like you bought the property next in 1990."

"Yes, I bought it from Jim Johnson. He decided to sell it after his wife passed away. He said the place reminded him of her too much so he had to move. He still lives over on Crabs Lake in a small cottage."

"I wonder if our mayor JJ is related to this Richard Jones? I'll have to ask him about that. Well, Judy, I want to thank you for your help. It's interesting to know some of the history of where you live."

I head back to the station to see what Rob has dug up. When I arrive there, I find him hunched over the computer. When I ask if he has found anything at all he replies, "I haven't found much at all. The courthouse probably has more info than I can get to."

"I just came from there and found out some history of the place. The only interesting thing was that the house was repossessed from a Richard Jones in 1971. I think I'm going to head over to the newspaper office and see if I can get some more history on that. I doubt there's any record of who built the house back in the early twenties. I'm also wondering if Richard Jones was related to our honorable mayor John Jones. I'll be back in a little while. Oh, I almost forgot. Did you happen to see anything in the papers at either house about the safes being built into the floors?'

"No, I didn't find anything in their papers at either place. I could go back and dig deeper in all their papers."

"Why don't you do that, Rob. I think it might pay to check with the close neighbors to see if they remember any carpenter work being done over the years. And one other idea I thought of. See if the safes are still open, which they should be. Get the brand, model number and serial numbers off of them. We might be able get ahold of the manufactures to get info on where they were sold to. It's a long shot, but you never know. I'm out of here, so I'll catch you later."

I head over to the local newspaper, which is located on main street. I laugh every time I see the paper's name. It's called *The Weekly Crow*. The owner and editor is Tom Finn. He's sitting at his desk when I walk in. When he sees me, he gets up quickly and comes over putting out his hand to shake mine.

"Duke Moran, as I live and breathe. I've been wanting to talk to you. You're a hard man to find. I'd love to get an interview with you about the murders. I haven't heard anything new lately."

"Well, Tom, there really isn't anything new to report. I can say we have a suspect in custody for the Betty Sagget murder. I think the chief is going to release some information in the morning. That's about all I can say right now."

"My reason for being here is to check on something for my own curiosity. I'm doing some history searching on my house. I've been to the courthouse and got info on past owners of the house. I'm been gradually remodeling it and thought I might see if any past owners were still around. The house has some interesting woodwork in it and I'd like to keep it through the whole house."

"What I'd like to see are copies of newspapers from 1970 to 1972 if possible. The house was owned by a guy named Richard Jones until 1971. But it shows the next owner bought it from the bank. I'm just curious as to what happened."

"Well, Duke, you came to the right person. I've lived here my whole life and I remember that story just like it happened yesterday. I was a teenager at the time and it was one of the biggest things to happen around here. That is until these two murders you're working on. I'm sure that our mayor Mr. Jones doesn't want this all dredged up again. Dick Jones was his grandfather, and it put a black mark on his family."

"This is the story as I heard it. Most of it is from what was stated in court and from various rumors going around. It's kind of pieces from here and there. So what's actually true and what's not is the question.

"It all started in August of 1970. I remember the month because it was hot as hell and so humid that you were drenched as soon as you got out of the shower. I was in my forties and was working here at the paper. My dad was still running the paper and I was reporting and also getting the ads."

"Dick Jones was living in your house with his wife JoAnn. They had one son named Jim. Jim had two sons named Scott and John. Scott was about ten years older than John. Of course, I'm sure you know of John, our mayor."

"Wait just a minute, you're saying John has a brother? I've never heard of him. Does he live around here?"

114

"I'm not sure where he is at this exact time. He was in prison and should still be there if he's still alive, but that's further into the story here."

"Dick Jones was a mean and nasty bastard, pardon my French. Word was that he beat his wife on a regular basis. And he was even worse on his son when he was growing up. He was a lumberjack and spent most of the weekdays up near the Canadian border cutting timber. He was also a drunk, or should I say a mean drunk. When he came home that's all he did."

"His son Charley stayed at home until he graduated from high school. He then moved out and got a job unloading the logger trucks at one of the many saw-mills up to the north of here. He eventually married his high school sweetheart, Annie, and had two kids. The kids, Scott and John were born ten years apart."

"Well, Jim was more mild-mannered like his mother. You would think all the beatings he got would have made him bitter. But I think his mother had a lot of influence on him. When he married Annie that seemed to be the best thing in the world for him."

"Scott was born about a year after they got married. And then John didn't come around until about ten years later. Everything seemed to go along pretty good for a number of years for Jim and his wife."

"When Scott got to be a little older, he started to become a problem. He was in fights at school and there started to be a lot of vandalism in the area. Rumor had it that Scott was behind a lot of it. But nothing could be pinned on him. He seemed to have inherited his grandpa Richards disposition."

"John on the other hand got along with everyone. He was younger but seemed to distance himself from his brother. You would very seldom see them together away from home."

"Then in, I believe in about 1968 Jim got killed. He was unloading a truck-load of logs. Apparently one of the side stakes holding the logs on the flatbed broke. They figure that when Jim undid one of the hold-down straps the load shifted. When one stake broke the rest along the line couldn't hold it all. Jim was standing on the ground on the side of the trailer and was crushed when the load let go. He was killed instantly."

"That meant that Jim's wife Annie needed to get a job. Jim had left a lot of bills that needed to be paid. She found a waitressing job at a local diner. This meant the two sons were left alone most of the time."

"Scott just kept getting into trouble and Annie couldn't control him at all. Scott spent a lot of time with his grandpa when he was home. They were like two peas in a pod. Eventually Dick invited Scott to come live with them. Annie didn't mind and I think it actually was a load off her mind. It made life much easier for her."

"Anyways, in August of 1970, I don't remember the exact day, is when everything started. Grandpa Dick was up north cutting down trees. Scott had gotten a job working in the old Molbray sawmill that was about twenty miles north of here. He had quit school the year before. Anyways Scott got into a fight with a coworker and his supervisor had sent him home early."

"It was the middle of the afternoon when he pulled into the driveway of grandpa and grandma's house He got out of his car and noticed another car sitting in front of the house. He didn't recognize it, but then he didn't pay much attention to who drove what."

"He went in the front door and was about to call out to his grandmother when he heard a sound in the back of the house. He heard a man's voice and then a woman giggling. It was coming from his grandparents' bedroom. Scott went to the dresser in his room and opened the bottom drawer. He pulled out his pistol that he kept hidden in there."

"He quietly went to the rear of the house. He heard more giggling, and he knew his granddad wasn't home. He went up to the door and quickly threw it open. There was his grandmother completely undressed in the arms of the most holy John Grisham who was also completely naked."

"John Grisham was the preacher at the local Baptist church. He was very popular in the community, always helping out where needed. He was also generous with his money, always donating where needed."

"So here he was in the arms of Scott's grandmother and apparently having his way with her. Scott raised the pistol and blew the Reverend Grisham's head off."

"Scott's grandmother JoAnn starts screaming her head off. Scott points the gun at her and tells her to shut up or he'll do the same to her."

"When she wouldn't stop screaming, Scott put the gun under her chin and pulled the trigger. He then put the gun in her right hand and got on the phone to call the police."

"When the police got there, they found Scott in the front room crying. Apparently, he had cleaned himself up before calling the police. You would think he'd gotten some blood on himself."

"Anyways they got him settled down enough to tell what happened. He told them that he came home early from work and heard the shots as he pulled up in his truck. He then ran into the house to find his grandmother and the preacher dead."

"They then put out phone calls to Grandpa Richard's employer to find him and send him home. It took a couple of hours to find him and send him home. He was out in the woods cutting down trees for the pulp mill."

"When Grandpa Richard got home and found out what had happened, he went into a rage. He started throwing anything he could get his hands on. It took, they say, five men to restrain him. They put him in handcuffs to protect himself and others around him."

"The police started to investigate the whole thing because there were some discrepancies in the facts of what happened."

"For one thing, JoAnn would have had to get out of bed to stand and kill the preacher John and then get back into bed and shoot herself. It was hard to believe she would get back in bed next to a dead man."

"They also found her with the gun in her right hand. The trajectory of the bullet under her chin was from her left to the right. That made sense being that she was actually left-handed. But the pistol was in her right hand, which made it impossible for her to make that shot. There's no way she could have switched the gun after she shot herself."

"Well, the police put two and two together and brought Scott in for questioning. It didn't take much to break min down into admitting the truth. In his mind he was doing the right thing in avenging his grandpa. So with Scott admitting to the killings, there wasn't really a trial. They had an inquest and then a brief hearing so his admission was on record and then they sentenced him. They gave him life in prison with no possible parole. A lot of folks thought he should have gotten a lighter sentence because of the circumstances. Messing with another man's wife was a cardinal sin to most people back then."

"Well, Scott went off to prison and Grandpa Richard went into a severe depression. He quit working and would sit on his front porch drinking and smoking all day. Things got back to normal and people went on with their daily routines. At some point not long down the road people happened to notice that Richard wasn't sitting on the porch anymore. It wasn't like people would stop and talk to him. He had always been so grouchy that people had always avoided him."

"Someone finally notice that Richard hadn't been seen out at all. They contacted the police who then went to the house. When they got no response, they called his daughter-in-law Annie to see if she had any knowledge of Richard's whereabouts. She said she hadn't talked to him much at all since Jim's death. She said Dick and her didn't get along much when Jim was alive, and afterward she wanted nothing to do with him."

"Next they got ahold of John his grandson to see if he had seen his grandfather. He also said he had nothing to do with Dick. The family had pretty much split up with Grandma's death and Scott in prison."

"So, the police decided to break in the house to make sure Richard was all right. They went to the house and broke a window in the door to unlock it. They did a thorough search, but found no one there. Next, they asked around town to see if anyone had seen Richard. They checked bars, grocery stores and even the barbershops. They eventually put out a missing person report to the whole state, plus Michigan, Minnesota, and Illinois."

"To this day no one knows what happened to Grandpa Richard Jones. There wasn't a lot of effort put into finding him. They figured he probably just took off to get away from the memories. When they checked out the house, they couldn't find any suitcases. So they figured he just took off."

"There was no will found, and there was a large mortgage on the house. The mortgage was because Richard borrowed on and off to buy things. And then took a bigger loan on it to pay for Scott's defense. There wasn't much of a defense, but they still had to get a lawyer for court. What money the lawyer didn't get Richard kept for his self to live on. He also had to pay to bury his wife, JoAnn. Apparently, he still loved her despite what she did."

"Now that I think about it there were two other men that also disappeared around the same time. They lived alone and were renting some old houses on the edge of town. They didn't associate with anyone much and just kept to themselves. Their clothes and everything were also gone, so it was assumed they just left town. All three men seemed to leave probably in the middle of the night. It was like they disappeared without a word."

"The names of the other two men were Johny Reid and Jack Humphrey. It seems strange now, but at the time they were pretty private men, so no one paid them much mind."

I thanked Tom for his time and the most interesting story. I was amazed that I hadn't heard all of this before. I think maybe the people around here just wanted to forget the whole thing.

I headed back to the police station to fill in Rob and the chief on what I'd just found out. I'm sure they'll agree that the body in my basement could be one of those three men. My guess would be Richard Jones is lying down there. He used to live there and nobody knows what happened to him. I'll have to ask our esteemed mayor what he knows about it. The million-dollar question is who killed him?

Back at the station after reporting my findings, I asked Rob, "What have you got on the safes? Did you find who installed them or who were the makers of them?"

"I did make some headway on them. Coincidently both safes are the same brand. They were both Gardall floor safes. They are headquartered in New York, and I got some information from them. I gave them the serial numbers on both units and found who bought them. The company sold them to Mecca Security Equipment located in Madison, Wisconsin. They have a warehouse on South Palm Street. Gardall also sent two more of the same floor safes to Mecca. So that's a total of four of the same safe sent to Mecca Security. They were all sold to them in August of 1985."

"I got ahold of someone at Mecca Security and asked about the installation of all four safes. They checked their records and found that three of them were sold in September of 1985 to a Bobby Brooks in our own town of Black Crow. They didn't know what type of work he did."

"We don't have a city directory here, but I did find his name in the county tax records. His address is 317 Maple Street. Taxes for last year were paid, so I assume he still lives there."

"Let's run over there and see him. I think it would be better in person in case he has records we can get from him. While we're out, I want to stop at both houses of the deceased and check on something."

So Rob and I jump in our car and go find Maple Street. We find the street and then the house. The street is only one-block long and lined on both sides with huge Maple trees. It's a very scenic block and you feel like you are driving through a tunnel. We pull up to a white colonial-style two-story house. It's trimmed in light blue and in mint condition. We go to the front door and ring the buzzer.

A very petite older lady comes to the door and asks if she can help us. She has gray hair and looks to be very fragile. We inform her that we are with the police department and would like to talk with Mr. Brooks. She looks at me, and I see a couple of tears coming from her eyes.

She says in a small voice, "My husband passed away about three months ago. He's been ill for most of the past year. I haven't even thought about clearing his things out of the house yet. After being married to him for the last sixty years, it's hard to imagine living without him."

"I'm sorry, what is it you needed my husband for? He's never been in trouble with the law that I know of."

"No, no he isn't or wasn't in trouble with the law. We just wanted to ask him about some woodworking jobs he might have done. He bought some floor safes back in 1985, and we wondered if he had records of what he did with them."

"Bobby probably installed them. He did a lot of carpentry on the side for people around the area for years. His main job was building houses for various contractors in the Black River Falls area. Unfortunately, I don't think he kept much in the way of records. Most of the work he did on the side was cash because most of the folks around here couldn't afford much. He did most of the jobs to help people out. You're welcome to check out his shop, which is in the back of our garage. He did have a couple of file cabinets back there that might have some records in them. I'll get the key and show it to you."

Mrs. Brooks got the key and had us follow through the house to the back door. The garage was separate from the house. We went down the back steps to the side door of the garage. The garage matched the house in style and color. It was much bigger than the house, though. It was a two-car garage, but was a double-deep building. There was a small overhead garage door on the back side with a service door next to it. Mrs. Brooks unlocked the service door and led us inside.

We walked into the small shop, which still smelled of sawdust. The room was about twenty-four by fifteen foot in size. It had your basic table saw, band saw, drill press, and a small lathe. You could see the shop was kept as clean as could be. It was swept up and the machines were clean. You could see sawdust on the items hanging all over. But all in all, it was pretty clean for a woodshop. He had a workbench that looked like he made it from a piece of butcher block countertop. In one corner there were two file cabinets. Even they had jigs and such piled on top of them.

I asked Mrs. Brooks if it was all right for us to look in them. She gave us the go-ahead. So we each opened one and started our search. The files dividers only had a number on them. There was a laminated sheet hanging on the wall which listed with a general idea of what the job was. Such as installed entry doors, installed garage door, installed new toilet or sink and so on. And there was a listing for safe installs. All these jobs were given a number starting with one hundred. Safe install was number 131. So, we went to the file cabinet that had a sign on it saying jobs. The other cabinet had a sign that said material orders.

We looked in the jobs cabinet under number 131. In that section we found manila folders with each year marked on them. There were only two folders in there for safe installation. So, we pulled the folders out and each took one.

I had the 1985 folder, and it had two invoices in it. They were for both the Anderson and Browning houses.

"Rob, I've got the invoices for the Anderson and Browning houses. They were installed in September and October of 1985."

"I've got another here in July of 1986. It was at 302 Pleasant Street in the town of Chaney. The homeowners name is under Jake Flowers."

"Well, Rob that shows where the three safes went to. We need to check out the house on Pleasant Street. Mrs. Brooks, is it all right if we take these invoices with us? We can get them back to you after we make copies."

"No, it's fine for you to keep them. I have no use for them. I actually need to box all this up and sell the tools. I just haven't been in a rush to get it done."

"It might be a good idea Mrs. Brooks to box and save them for a few years in case something like this comes up again. Your husband kept very good records the way it looks here."

"I'll make sure I do that. Is there anything else you might need?"

"No, I think we're fine, Mrs. Brooks, and we would like to thank you for helping us out. We are really sorry to hear about your husband's passing."

We left the garage and got into our car. I figured we should go check out the Pleasant Street house. On our way to the Pleasant Street address, I informed Rob of my reason for wanting to check something in both murder scenes.

"I've been thinking that the murderer slash thief had to have a way to get the safes open quickly. The only answer I come up with is that he knew the combination. And the only way to get them is either the people told him or he saw the safes being opened."

"He could have done some business deal with them that might involve them getting something out of the safe. Which of course the killer would have to be standing there watching. And if that was the case why not just murder them right there. That seems pretty far-fetched."

"My other thought is that the killer somehow had a camera hidden that would be motion activated. He would have had to be able to mount it quickly without their knowing it. Which would mean he needed a reason to be in their homes. They'd definitely have to know him personally or have some service-related job."

"I want to go over those closets with a fine-tooth comb. With some luck, maybe we can find some small clue."

We arrive at 302 Pleasant Street at five o'clock. The house is your typical Cape Cod house. It has a steep roof with slate siding and window shutters. The color is robin's egg blue with white trim. It's in excellent shape and the small yard is neatly trimmed and looks weed free. These people have taken very good care of the place. We get out of the car and start to walk up to the front door. We hear some pounding coming from the area of the garage, which is in the back and side of the house. So, we turn and go around the house to the garage.

We get to the back and see an elderly looking man nailing some two by fours together. We walk up and call out to him. He's startled and jumps at our calling. After turning and seeing us he says we surprised him. We apologize and inform him that we're with the police department. He asks what he can do for us.

I say, "I take it your Jake Flowers? We're investigating the recent murders that happen in the area and would like to ask you some questions."

"Sure, I'd be happy to do anything I can do to help. Although I don't know what I would know that could help you. I didn't know the unfortunate folks that were killed. Why don't we sit down on the deck there and talk? Might just as well sit and be comfortable while we talk. Can I get either of you any-thing to drink first?"

"No, thanks, Mr. Flowers, we're just fine. You can get yourself something if you wish."

"No, I'm just fine. I've learned at my age to take it easy. I don't work any harder than I have to. And you can call me Jake. We're not too formal in our house."

"I'll get right to the point, then. We understand you have a built-in floor safe in your house. It was installed by Bobby Brooks in 1985. We're just check-ing out different leads and your safe came up. It was one of three that were in-stalled by Mr. Brooks in the same time period. Has anyone ever brought up the subject of your safe or has it ever been broken into?"

"We've had no trouble at all here. I had the safe put in mainly in case we have a fire that our records will be safe. I do keep some money in there, but it's only a couple of thousand dollars."

"Have you had any service people doing any work in the house for you in the past year? Such as repair work on anything or something new put in?"

"No, nothing has been done in the last year unless it was done by my own hands. Nothing major has broken down. and I fix the small things myself."

"Well, we thank you for your time. If you happen to see anything strange or someone that seems odd in the area please let us know. You have also done a great job of keeping the house up all these years."

"Oh, wait a minute; I don't know if this means anything. Mr. Brooks had a young man helping him put the safe in. It was relatively heavy and took two of them just to get it in the house. And then they had to lower it into the floor. I didn't know the young man or his name. It probably doesn't help you any, but I thought I should mention it"

"Well, you never know, Mr. Flowers, but we will check it out. Thanks again and enjoy the rest of the day."

"Well, Rob, I think we had better stop back and see Mrs. Brooks. Hopefully Mr. Brooks kept a record of paying any helpers he had."

We get back to the Brooks' house and knock on the door. When Mrs. Brooks answers I ask if she remembers Mr. Brooks having any young men help him out. She said he did get help once in a while when the job was more than he could handle alone.

"I don't remember any of their names, but I'm sure there's something in the shop files. You're welcome to go back there and check it out."

We get the keys and head back out to the shop. Once inside I tell Rob to go through the desk while I hit the file cabinets. There should be some records of paying any help for tax purposes.

After about forty-five minutes of searching, I found invoices for materials purchased and paid for. But I found nothing about paying anyone.

"Rob, have you found anything in the desk? I'm guessing that Mr. Brooks was paying any help he had under the table. It makes sense if he very seldom needed help. The paperwork would have not have been worth the trouble."

"Duke, I think I found something here. He had a book here for phone numbers and there's a sheet of paper in it with names on it. Here take a look and see what you think."

"There are about ten names with phone numbers listed. There's the word help written in one of the top corners. I bet this is his call list for part-time help. Most of the names have been crossed off. I'm sure that with time they found other full-time jobs, so Mr. Brooks had to come up with new help. I don't know how old this list is, so I think we need to start at the top and check each name out. Hopefully we can narrow down who was helping him in 1985."

We returned the keys to Mrs. Brooks and thanked her again for her help.

Once back in the car, I told Rob to go to the Anderson house first. I did remember to grab keys to both houses when we left the station. I figured it wouldn't take long to check out the closet of both houses. I was getting hungry, and it was five o'clock, so hopefully this wouldn't take long. And I told Rob that maybe we could start some preliminary checks on the names after supper.

We arrived at the Anderson house and grabbed a couple of flashlights. Once inside we went right to the closet. We searched every inch of the walls and the shelving. Underneath and all corners. We didn't even find a single hole or any evidence of something stuck on any surface.

So we left there and went to the Browning residence and had the same results. We then headed back to the station. Once at the station, I told Rob I was going to go get a bite to eat at Barb's. I asked if he wanted to go along. He said he would like to get started on checking out the names through the computer. He asked me to pick him up a sandwich. I agreed and left to eat.

I returned back to the station about an hour later to find Rob still working away on the computer.

"How's it going, Rob? Made any progress? Why don't you take a break to eat and fill me in on what you've found out so far?"

"Sounds good to me Duke. I think I've narrowed it down to two people who helped Mr. Brooks in 1985. They are the fifth and sixth names on the list."

"The fifth name is, and get this, Jack Sampson. Is that a coincidence, or what? And the sixth name is a Josh Andrews. I was just going to call Josh Andrews to find out where he lives now. I found a phone number for him in the white pages on the computer."

"Why don't you eat your sandwich and I'll call him."

The phone rings about ten rings, and I'm thinking no one is going to answer. Just before I go to hang up, someone picks up on the other end. It's a woman who answers. I inform her of who I am and ask for Josh Andrews.

She says, "I'm the former Mrs. Andrews. We were divorced a year ago."

"This is the phone number we found for him. Do you have a newer phone number for him? We have some questions for him having to do from 1985."

"I'm afraid I don't have a number for him. After the divorce went through, he up and took off. We have two children and I haven't received a cent of child support from him. I have no idea where he went and the state child support agency can't find him either. I do know that he quit his job before he left, and he had already cleaned out our checking and savings accounts before the divorce. It's all kind of odd because he was a good provider during our first five years of marriage. But in the end, he started staying out late nights and I found out he was cheating on me."

"So if you happen to find where he is, I would appreciate if you could let me know. I've had my hands full raising and supporting the three of us."

"I will definitely let you know if we find him. Where are you from so we have somewhere to start our search. I'm calling from northern Wisconsin."

"I'm from Independence, Missouri. I don't think Josh is living around here. I would think the state would have found him by now. If they do find him, they said they'd go after him for back child support."

"Did he do something wrong back in 1985?"

"No, we're just checking on some employment he had with a man back then. I thank you for your time and information, and if we find him, I will let you know. If you think of anything else please feel free to call me at 608-514-8612 and ask for Duke or Rob. Thanks again."

"Well, Rob there's another thing to add to our list of things to check out. Tomorrow I'm going to go talk to Sampson in his cell. I doubt he'll be very forthcoming with any answers, but you never know. I'm beat so I think it's time to get some sleep."

I suggested we meet up at the station in the morning and cover what we found out with the chief. I said that after we meet with the chief in the morning, he could probably start the fingerprint and inventory search of the evidence in my basement. I told him he would need to grab some evidence bags from the storeroom. I happened to see some in there when we did the interrogations. They looked pretty old as there was a ton of dust on them. I guess there wasn't a lot of use for them in our small town.

So I headed home and decided to see if the Brewers game was on TV.

I grabbed a beer from the refrigerator and went to turn on the television. I was trying to find if the Brewers game was on when there was a knock at the door. I get up to answer it and see it is Rick Turner, the chief's son.

I open the door and invite him in. He tells me that he has a camera for the back door and would like to hook it up. So we go to the back door, and I throw my sandwich into the refrigerator as we pass. Rick apologizes about interrupting my meal. I tell him its fine as it's just a cold sandwich.

Rick says, "I want to apologize about the other night. I was way out of line and had too much to drink. I assure you it won't happen again."

"Okay, Rick, let's forget it and start over. It's not worth spending any more time on it."

I show him the back door in the kitchen and point out the pane that keeps getting broken. Rick looks around and points to the shelves above the stairway leading to the basement. There are boxes and spare cooking pans cluttered up there. He says it would be a perfect place to hide the camera.

We decide to use a box and cut a small hole in it and place the camera inside it. He says the camera was on loan from a buddy of his in the local FBI office in Madison. They had just got this new model in and hadn't had a chance to try them out yet. The camera unit was about two in by two-inch square. It had a small antenna on the back that stuck up about three inches. He said it was motion activated and would send a signal to a receiver that recorded what set it off. He said it would take a picture each time it was activated.

Then we just had to plug the receiver into a computer laptop he had to see the pictures. He said the battery in the camera should last about a week if it didn't have to take a ton of pictures. Then we can switch the batteries for fresh recharged ones. We can hide the receiver somewhere in your house so no one sees it. I'll come back in about five days to check it out if you don't have any more broken windows before then.

So we got the camera in place and put the receiver in one of the kitchen cabinets. Then we tried it out to see if it would work. I came in the back door and then Rick fired up his laptop. He found the app he had installed and next thing you know there was a picture of me coming in the back door.

So I thanked Rick and went back to find my ballgame and beer. I spent the rest of the night on the couch and eventually fell asleep watching the Brewers lose another game.

Chapter 21

. . . .

Wednesday June 26

I woke up with the sun shining in my eyes. It took me a minute to figure out where I was. I manage to sit up and finally climb to my feet. I went out to the kitchen and got the coffee pot started. I still have one of those old metal percolator coffee pots with the strainer in it. I think that they make the best coffee you can get.

Anyways I hit the shower to get awake and manage to down a couple of cups of coffee. My next stop is the cop shop.

I get to the station at about eight o'clock. I grab another cup of coffee. although it's not as good as mine. I also grab a couple of donuts, that are just sitting there, to get my sugar rush. Then I head into the conference room to find the chief and Rob already there with their coffee and donuts.

Rob and I go through everything we did yesterday with the chief and tell him we don't really have any more clues as to who the murderer is. I mention that, "I'm going to stop at the jailhouse and ask Sampson if he worked for Bobby Brooks in 1985. I doubt he'll be very forthcoming with any info, but it's worth a try."

"I think our next step is for Rob to start checking for fingerprints and boxing up the cash and jewelry in my basement. Maybe we'll get lucky and he finds something to help us."

As I get ready to leave the chief reminds me, "Duke, you have to be in court tomorrow morning for both Sampson and Sagget pretrial hearings. Both you and Rob need to be there to give testimony."

Rob replies to me, "While you go talk to Sampson, I'm going to do a little searching on the computer to see if I can get a lead on where Josh Andrews might be. Let me know when you are ready to go to your house."

I went to see Jack Sampson in his jail cell. I didn't see any reason to get him out and have to wait for his lawyer. I basically wanted to see if he worked for Bobby Brooks back in 1985.

The jail is in the rear of the police station. So I just had to walk through a security door to get there. There's a guard in an office, and before you go in, you have to sign a log book and he takes any weapons you might have. The jail is uncommonly clean. They keep any inmates they have busy cleaning in and around the police station. Most inmates are in for minor infractions. Any prisoners such as Sampson are not let out to do cleanup work.

I approach Sampson's cell and catch him asleep. I call out his name to awaken him. He slowly awakens and looks up at me. Apparently, he's not happy to see me. He starts cussing at me and telling me to get the hell out of his sight.

I reply, "Now come on, Jack. There's no need to be that way. I just came to see how you are getting on. You'll get your say tomorrow in front of the judge. I have just one simple question and it has nothing to do with your case."

"Why should I answer any of your questions? I'm not going to get anything for it."

"That's true, but it's not going to hurt you either. And maybe I'll be a little more on your side when we go to court. And my question is a simple one. All I want to know is if you worked for a Bobby Brooks back in 1985."

"I didn't really work for him. He called one day for some help, and I went over to his place. He said what he had to do and started ordering me around. He had this heavy safe he expected me to pick it up and carry to his truck. I asked for a hand truck and he said he didn't have one. I said it would take two people to carry it and he got all bent out of shape. He said he couldn't lift it himself because of his back. I said if I lift it, I won't have a back left. Then I asked where it was going. He said it was going in an upstairs bedroom. Well, I told him there was no way I was carrying it up a flight of stairs. So I told him to shove his job and walked out."

"I went home and got to thinking. I could really use some money as I was broke. So I borrowed a two-wheel cart from our neighbor and headed back to Brooks' place. Well, I drove in front of his house and saw movement in front of his garage. Here was a kid about my age with a hand cart hauling the safe to the back of Brook's truck. Well, that really frosted my ass, so I went back home."

"Did you happen to know the kid that was helping Brooks?"

"No, I didn't know his name but had seen him around town every so often."

"Well, thanks, Jack. Is there anything you need here to make your stay any better?"

"No, I have all the comforts of home. Unless you can sneak a television in here."

"I don't think they would let me get away with that. Thanks for the help, and I'll see you tomorrow."

I went back to the front to collect Rob and head to my house. We grabbed some evidence bags and his fingerprinting kit and headed out.

On the way I asked Rob if he got any leads on the whereabouts of Josh Andrews.

"Not really. I got a copy of his Missouri driver's license. I also got his social security number. I've got a request in to the social security department to see if he's got a job where they're drawing his social security tax from. Hopefully we hear something from them today. He had one incident with the Kansas City police for drunken fighting at a bar. But it was from before the divorce. I thought that next I'd call his ex-wife back and see if I can get the names of any buddies he might have."

"Well, that's a good start. Hopefully we can get some leads soon. I have this funny feeling that we haven't seen the last of our killer yet. I'd like to catch him before he does anything else. If he hits again, we won't be able to keep Madison and the FBI out of this."

"Why would the FBI get into it? It's just happening in Wisconsin."

"Another killing and it will be classified as a serial killing. Then the FBI will have to be called in."

We got to my house, and I helped Rob get the gear down into the basement. We then got the shelving pulled out of the way and the door to the hidden room opened up. It's kind of an eerie feeling to have a completely decomposed body sitting there in plain sight.

"Rob, will it bother you having that body sitting there? I hate to get the coroner in here yet and tip off the suspect that we might onto him."

"No, it's fine. There's no smell and I'll just try to avoid looking at it. I probably wouldn't hurt to put another tarp over it. That one's pretty holey."

"I just happen to have some brand-new ones out in the garage. They're still sealed in the wrapper so they won't contaminate the corpse. I'll go get one."

I got the body covered up and told Rob I was going to go finish painting my upstairs bathroom. It would give me some time to think and get some work done.

I got the paint out and got to work on the bathroom. It only took me about half an hour to finish up. I was standing there admiring my handiwork when the phone started to ring.

It was the chief calling. He said, "There was a hit on a piece on jewelry from one of the murder/burglaries. A pawnshop in Madison received a diamond necklace that matches one on the stolen list that was sent out. They recognized it because the necklace was custom made. I told them we would come down there and get any information he might have."

"Would you and Rob mind running down there in the morning? They're supposed to document information on people they do business with. Maybe they have cameras that will show us the suspect. This could be our first real lead. At least I hope it is."

"This sounds good. I'll talk to Rob and set up our departure time. I remember when I was on the police force in Madison that the pawnshops had to record info from a driver's license or ID. With that and maybe some video, we might get a break. So wish us luck, Chief."

I went downstairs to Rob and told him the situation and to be ready to leave at eight o'clock in the morning. He said he'd be ready to go then. I also told him to wear civilian clothes instead of his usual police uniform. He seems to prefer the uniform over civilian clothes. I think he hopes it gives him an advantage with the ladies. Seeing as how he is single, I guess it doesn't hurt to try anything.

He said he'd finished the fingerprinting and would save boxing the rest up for later. So far he hadn't found any prints.

Chapter 22

. . . .

Thursday June 27

I got up at six thirty and hit the shower right away. It was going to be a long day with the drive and driving in all that traffic in Madison. I've gotten used to the quiet empty roads of a small town.

I forgot to fill the tank with gas yesterday, so my first stop was Hamme's Beer and Gas. I don't know where he came up with that name. But the two seemed to go with each other. The station was pretty run-down, in need of a fresh coat of paint. It was a pretty small building, but half of it was coolers filled with beer. The other half was a small counter with an old cash register and some shelves with snacks piled on them.

None of the merchandise had prices on it or on the shelf. Hamme always said if you have to ask the price you can't afford it. Plus, there was no rhyme or reason to how the snacks were placed on the shelves. It was pretty much just stacked where there was room. Hamme said he didn't have time on his hands to stack things neat. Funny thing was all he ever did was sit in his chair behind the counter. I don't think anyone has ever seen him on his feet. If you happened to be in there when he got a delivery, he'd ask you to open the box and throw it on the shelf anywhere.

And grooming wasn't one of Hamme's strong suits. He had a straggly beard and his clothes always looked like he'd slept in them. He always had a weird smell on him. Back then I didn't know what it smelled like. But as I got older and spent more than my share of time in taverns, I figured it out. He was always nipping at the bottle. He was a friendly enough of a guy but always let you know he had an answer for everything. When I was a kid, I'd ask him stupid questions just to see what answer he'd come up with. Nobody new how old he was, but I swear he hadn't aged since I was a kid. He once told me I was a pain in his prostate. At that time, I didn't even know what a prostate was.

Well, I filled the gas tank and went in to pay Hamme. I also grabbed some snacks for breakfast and later on the road. As I paid Hamme, I asked him why it was that women could breast feed and men couldn't. Of course, he remembered who I was and how I always asked him dumb questions. The look he gave me made my insides quiver. I swear there was fire coming out of those eyes.

But he calmly replies to me, "When you learn to squat and piss then you'll be able to breast feed. Now, if that's all you need, I need to get back to work."

I stopped and picked Rob up at his apartment at eight o'clock, and we headed out on the road. It was a beautiful day for a drive. The temperature was around seventy-five degrees with very few clouds in the sky. It's about a ninety-minute drive to Madison.

Rob said this was the first time he got to get out of town doing investigating work. He told me he hadn't ever done much traveling in his life. He took correspondence courses on police science and got the bug to be a detective. He also took a few classes at Madison Technical College to complete his degree. He said he always liked to try and figure out puzzles.

I asked Rob, "Have you ever thought about getting a job in a larger police department, to get more experience? There's a larger variety of crimes to investigate. It sounds like that would be right up your alley."

"I thought about that and did check it out. The problem is you have to start out as a patrolman and work your way up to detective. It can take quite a few years to get to detective as I'm sure you know. It might be small-time in Black Crow, but I get to mix police and detective work together. I admit I don't get to work on many big profile cases, but I enjoy what I'm doing."

"Well, I kind of envy you, Rob; it's rare to find someone who actually likes their job. I do like my life now, but it wasn't always that way."

"Anyways, the chief said we're to see a Ralph Gunther at State Street Pawnshop in Madison. It's a favorite place for the college kids to get quick cash. He should have a name and address for us. By law they have to get that information from people bringing items to pawn. I'll take the lead in questioning Mr. Gunther. If you think of any questions, don't be afraid to jump in.

I've got a feeling that this is going to lead to something. It's the first break we've gotten so far."

We hit the outskirts of Madison at ten thirty and got off Interstate 90 to head downtown. State Street runs off the square downtown where the state capitol is.

We find State Street and drive until we find the pawnshop address. We lucked out to find a parking space in front of the pawnshop. It's a pretty decent-looking building. A lot of pawnshops I've seen over the years are pretty run-down. It has two huge picture windows facing the street and they're packed with various merchandise. Anything from mannequins to pet animals are squeezed in there. There had to be at least a thousand items in each window. It was cluttered, but at the same time interesting to check out. We found ourselves standing there pointing out the various things.

Rob and I walked in the front door. There were literally thousands more items crammed into the place. Shelves were full and various items are hanging from the ceiling throughout the store. Straight down the main aisle we see a caged-in area. It was like the old-fashioned bank teller cages. It was like we stepped back in time.

Sitting behind the cage we could see a big man. And he gets even bigger the closer we get to him. As we get up to the cage, we see he is massive. He has to weigh in at around three hundred pounds plus. I can't even see the chair he's sitting on because his massive body blocks everything.

I was at first speechless, and then I finally found my voice. "Hello, I'm Duke Moran and this is Rob Turner. We're detectives from the Black Crow police department and our chief told us you received a piece of jewelry we might be looking for. It was listed on the stolen jewelry list we sent out around the state. I have a picture of it that we got from the insurance company. It along with some other jewelry was taken in a murder/burglary case we're working on."

"We were told to see a Ralph Gunther here. Would that happen to be you?"

"Yes, that's me. Do you have some identification to prove who you are?"

"Sure we do, here you go. My badge is from my time on the Madison PD. I'm helping the Black Crow police solve two double murders. Rob here is from the Black Crow police department as you can see from his ID."

"Okay, I believe who you are. Can I see the picture of the piece you think I might have? I'll need it to compare with what I have here."

"Here's the picture. It's a custom-made piece, so we're told. It's supposed to be one of a kind."

I hand the picture to Mr. Gunther and he says, "It looks like the piece I took in. Hold on and let me go get it out of my safe."

Gunther climbs off his stool and goes into the back of the store. I was hoping that he didn't have a heart attack walking that far. He was definitely overweight and out of shape.

Gunther came back after a few minutes and laid the piece of jewelry on the counter. I laid the picture next to it and it was a perfect match. I turned the piece over and the jewelers mark on the back matched the other picture I had.

I said, "Mr. Gunther, we're going to have to take this piece with us. It's evidence in a double murder. I'll give you a receipt for it and with any luck maybe you can recover your money when we catch the person that sold it to you."

"Now, aren't you supposed to keep a record of who brings merchandise in to you? And I see you have security cameras all around here. We need to see if you caught the person on tape so we can identify them."

"Here's my log book that I keep the records in. I just need the number off the tag on the necklace. What number do you have on it?"

"It looks like 024867. Your penmanship is pretty bad."

"I can read it and that's all that counts. I received the necklace last week on Thursday. I gave him four hundred dollars for it. He wanted a lot more, but I figured it might be hot. I know how hard it is to get your money back when the police take things in for evidence. He must have been really desperate for money. We bartered back and forth and he finally settled for the four hundred."

"So what's his name and do you have him on camera?"

"I took this off his driver's license. The name I have is Jake Knowles. His address is 123 Mill Pond Road in Black Crow, Wisconsin. Is this guy really a murderer? I don't want him coming back here for causing him trouble."

"Don't worry about him coming back. Once we get him, he won't be going anywhere. And the necklace is stolen, but we don't know for sure if this guy actually committed the murders. So let's get a look at what you have on your cameras. Does your system keep recordings for a week?"

"Yes, it does. I save the tapes for about a year. In this business it pays to cover all bases."

"That's great. Let's see if we can get a picture of this guy."

"Okay, why don't you guys go around to the side there and I'll let you in that door.

He lets us in and we go towards the rear of the store. Mr. Gunther has us go into a small office back there.

I ask Gunther, "Aren't you afraid of someone sneaking in the front door while your back here?"

He says, "Not to worry, I have a switch on the door that alerts me to anyone coming in. Plus, I have cameras covering most of the store. I've been in the business long enough to know to cover my ass. Now here's the recording setup."

The three of us are crammed into Gunther's small office. Of course, he takes up half the room himself. On one wall there's a desk with papers scattered all over. Another wall has four file cabinets lined up side by side. The third wall has a shelf unit with six small screen televisions on it. They are all showing different parts of the store. There is a VCR hooked up to each set. Gunther explains that the cameras are motion activated. Once they sense movement they start recording and keep recording for fifteen minutes once movement stops.

"Then as the tapes get full, I date them and store them away in the storeroom. I'll go get the tapes for last Thursday and we can watch on this spare television."

Gunther left the office and went into a room across the hall. Of course, we had to back out of the office to let him out and back in.

He returned with two VCR tapes. We all packed back into his office. Luckily, he has air-conditioning, otherwise it would get pretty uncomfortable in this office.

Gunther turns on the spare television and pops in one of the tapes. He said it was the one for the camera showing people standing at his cage window. He explains there's a time stamp that shows on the screen while it plays.

The time stamp shows Thursday the 20th of June. Gunther fast-forwards to twelve o'clock for that day. He then slows it down to normal speed. We can then see a rough-looking guy come to the window. The guy looks like a homeless person. His hair is unruly and filthy. His clothes are rumpled and look like they haven't seen a washing machine in ages. He also has a straggly beard.

There's no sound with the recording so we can't hear what his voice sounds like. I ask Rob if he recognizes the man. He says he doesn't and I've never seen him either.

We watch as the guy lays a necklace on the counter for Gunther to look at. Gunther picks it up and carefully inspects it. The two men are talking back and forth. At one point, Gunther slides the necklace back to the guy shaking his head no. Then the guy makes a gesture with his hands and shakes his head yes. He then pulls a billfold from his pocket and hands what looks like a driver's license to Gunther.

Gunther then writes in his log book and counts out some money which he hands to the man. The man then turns and walks out of sight.

I ask Gunther, "Do you have any cameras outside in front of the store that show any cars sitting there? Maybe we could see him get in a car if he has one."

"No, I don't have any cameras in the front of the store. I only have one in the rear of the building. I figure if someone tries to break in it will be back there out of sight."

I ask Gunther for a copy of the tape. He tells me to take the original. If he has any need of it, he will call us.

I fill out a receipt for the necklace and recorded tape for Gunther. We thank him and tell him that we will let him know the outcome of our investigation.

We get back into our car and head back to the interstate. Rob says his stomach is starting to growl. I suggest we stop at an all-you-can-eat buffet called Heritage House. It's on our way out of the city and I know Rob can really put away the food. He says it sounds good to him.

We get to the Heritage House and pay inside the door. I then show Rob to one of the buffet lines. I'm watching Rob fill his plate as we go down the line. He has food stacked a mile high on his plate. It's going to start sliding off the plate if he keeps filling it. I let him know that he can make as many trips to the food as he wants. He says that he's afraid they might run out of food. I reassure him that won't happen.

Rob eats everything on his plate so fast that he could be mistaken for a vacuum cleaner. He starts to get out of his chair and I ask where he's going.

"I'm still hungry so I'm going to get another plateful. Do we have enough time left?"

"Sure, we have plenty of time, Rob. I hope you have extra holes in your belt so you can let it out. That's a lot of food you're putting away."

When he gets back, I see he overfilled his plate again. I then got up to get some dessert and told Rob I'd be right back.

When I get back to the table, I noticed Rob's plate was empty again. He gets up and says he's going to get some dessert. I was getting full just looking at all the food Rob had eaten.

When he returns to the table, I see his plate is overflowing with desserts. He sat down and cleaned his plate again. I thought I was going to be sick thinking of all that food he'd eaten. The guy should weigh at least three hundred pounds. But he's as skinny as a rail.

I asked, "Do you always eat this much food? I've never seen anybody put away that much food before. I hope you're finally done."

"Yes, I'm done. I grew up with two older brothers and they would always steal my food. So, I had to learn to eat fast and get as much as I could get. I usually tried to get to the dinner table before my brothers so I could fill my plate. It got to be a game after a while. We would try to come up with phony reasons to keep each other from getting to the table. Such as telling them one of their buddies was waiting down the street for them or something on that order."

"So, are you full enough so we can head back to Black Crow? I think we should check out the address we got before dark. I'm surprised we haven't ever spotted this Jack Knowles around the Black Crow area before. You'd think he would stand out by the looks of him. I've never seen anyone that filthy around our area. Plus, you would think he'd spent some time in jail or at least getting arrested for something. I even checked with Jim Knowles from the coffee clutch, and they're not related."

"Okay, Duke, I'm full and ready to roll. And I haven't seen anyone like him around either. There aren't really that many permanent residents in our area. I figure I know the majority of the people either by name or on sight. After all I've lived there my whole life. I delivered newspapers as a kid to the whole town at one time or another. I also don't remember many houses on Mill Pond Road or any of the people living there. I guess we'll know soon enough."

"You know, Rob, I don't see this Jack Knowles as the type of person that could have gotten enough knowledge about the Anderson and Browning homes. I doubt they would have invited him into their homes. But we definitely need to find him. If he isn't the one that did the killing, he had to get the necklace from whoever did it. We should hopefully find something out soon."

We pull into Black Crow around three o'clock. I figured we had better stop at the station first and get some backup. We also needed to fill the chief in on what we found out. We didn't know what to expect out on Mill Pond Road.

The chief is in his office when we walk in. We knock and he motions us in. I fill him in on what we found out in Madison. I hand over the necklace, which I had put in and evidence bag. I also give him the tape, which he sticks in his tape player. I tell him what time to fast forward to. He finds the shot of Jack Knowles and freezes on it.

"Duke, is this for real? This guy looks like a homeless person. His driver's license shows an address on Mill Pond Road?"

"Yes, that's what Gunther took off the guy's driver's license. I thought we'd better take back up with us. After that fiasco out at that old farm we need to not take any chances."

"You're right, Duke. I'll get us two more cars to go along. That will make five of us. That's going to have to do it. Is there any way we can print some pictures from this so everyone knows what Jake Knowles looks like?"

"Rob, why don't you take a picture with your camera and we'll run it to the drug store and see how quick they can make some copies."

About twenty minutes later, Rob got back from the drugstore.

"We can't get copies of the picture until tomorrow. It's too late in the day for them to start the machine up and the person that does it is gone for the rest of the day."

"Okay, then, we'll go without. At least some of us know what he looks like," replies the chief.

Once everyone is rounded up, we head out and jump in our cars. We have a mini convoy going out to Mill Pond Road, which is about two miles out of Black Crow.

We get to Mill Pond Road and drive along looking for number 123. We find numbers 101 and 131. It's the only two mailboxes on this block. The block is about a mile long, so we decide to split up and walk the area between the two mailboxes. It's all woods on that side of the road. Rob shouts out that he found what looks like a driveway. I radio the chief to bring everyone to where Rob is.

Everyone gathered together where Rob found the driveway going into the woods. It's not much of a driveway. The grass is two-foot high and the trees spread out enough to narrow the driveway up. It doesn't look like it's been used in quite a while.

We decide to walk in instead of trying to drive it. That way no one will hear us coming and we will have the element of surprise on our side. We start walking in, two wide with our guns ready. We all have shotguns and the two AR15's the force has. We all also had our side arms strapped to our sides.

We didn't rush our way getting in. We were trying to see through the trees for any buildings or people. After we had walked about a quarter of a mile, we could see some buildings in the distance. We stopped short of the buildings to rest up and come up with a plan of attack. It was rough walking in. The road was full of deep ruts and being covered with tall grass made it tough walking. Plus, the tree branches kept smacking us in the head.

We decided to have three of us go and surround the area on all sides. Two of us (the chief and I) would go in from the front. Then one officer would go around to the right side and one the left. The third would go around to the rear. Once in place we would converge on all four buildings.

There was the house on the left, an oversized garage sat next to it. Then another pole shed that looked like it might hold machinery for fieldwork. And a barn was on the right.

The place looked and felt deserted. The house was an old two-story farmhouse. It is falling apart with peeling paint. The whole structure was leaning badly to the left. It didn't look safe to even go in.

The barn looked the most solid of the whole place. It was going to be awkward to check each building and watch the others at the same time.

The chief decided that the two of us would start with the house while the others tried to keep an eye on the other buildings and cover our backs.

The chief called out, "If anyone's in the house, come out with your hands up. We have you covered on all sides. This is the Black Crow police department."

When he got no answer, we decided to rush the house. There wasn't much for cover between us and the house. So we each took off for each side of the house on a fast run. We did not have bulletproof vests that a lot of the big police departments were getting. They're expensive, and Black Crow has a tight budget.

We covered the roughly one hundred feet to the two trees in front of the house without getting shot at. I shouted to Rob, who was in the rear of the buildings to watch the back of the house. Then the chief and I ran to the front door.

I whisper to the chief to be careful. The floor inside the house might not be safe. We should probably stay close to the walls. He agrees and we walk into the porch at the front of the house. I grab ahold of the chief's arm and point down. The floor is already got a hole in it. We then step very carefully on the floor joists to get to the doorway. The door is actually lying on the floor. It looks like it was ripped away from the frame.

We look into the kitchen and see a real mess. The cupboards are all hanging at odd angles ready to fall off the walls and the paint is peeling off all over the place. The house feels like it's moving as we try to go to the next room.

I say, "Chief, I think we'd better get out of here. The whole house seems to be moving. I can't see anyone having been in here for years. I do see some old mail lying on the counter and floor over there by the window. I'm going to try and get some of it to check the address and name on it."

I slowly worked my way around the kitchen, using the countertop to take some of my weight off the floor. I get within reach of the mail on the counter and grab a handful. Then I recede back to the door and get out with the chief.

When we get outside, I glance at the mail. The address shows 123 Mill Pond Road. The name shows Art Knowles.

"Chief, we've got the right address. The mail is addressed to an Art Knowles. My guess is he might be Jake's father. The date stamped on this mail by the post office is from three years ago. It also seems to be mostly junk mail. I really doubt anyone had been staying in this house. We should probably get the rest of the buildings checked out and see what we can find."

"Sounds like a good idea, Duke. Why don't we start with the garage first? It's close and will only take a minute to check out."

We run over to the garage where one of the extra officers is waiting. He says everything seems quiet. The garage was only about twenty foot by twenty foot. It had the old swing open doors. One officer and I each took a door and pulled them open quickly while the chief had his gun ready.

There was a 1956 Chevrolet sitting in there. We checked it out and found it empty. I popped the trunk open and found it empty. The car had tons of rust all over it and all the tires were flat. Apparently, it hadn't been moved for years.

Next, we went over to the other building, which was bigger in size. It was a pole shed about forty foot by eighty foot. We couldn't see a service door, so we had to slide the big main door to the side to open it.

We all get ready with guns ready and slide the door open. It's full of old farming equipment. There's an old three-row corn picker. I also saw a plow, disc, and corn planter. There was also a lot of other older, probably unusable equipment.

We made a quick pass through the place to no avail. We found nothing living in there.

So next was to head over to the barn. We didn't expect to find anything, but we still weren't taking any chances. Rob was waiting for us at the front of the barn.

"Rob, have you heard anything coming from inside the barn? The house seems to be empty. It's unsafe to even be in there."

"No. I haven't heard a thing. It's actually too quiet out here. The whole place seems deserted and desolate."

"How many doors have you seen to get in here Rob?"

"There's this huge earthen ramp that goes up to the slide-open doors for the haymow. Then I saw a normal-size Dutch-style door on the right side. It was closed up and seemed to be locked. I did go to the other side, and there's a big open doorway that has an animal pen hooked on the outside. It probably held a few animals at one time. I didn't see any door on the back side at all."

"Okay, let's split up. John, you guard that locked door, Rob and Terry keep an eye on this door up at the top of the ramp, then the Chief and I will go around to the open side doorway. Okay, let's get to it."

The chief and I went around to the side and found a spot where the fence had been trampled down. We entered the barn with guns ready. We got inside and found it empty. There wasn't even a bale of hay in it.

We found a ladder that went up into the haymow. We radioed to the others that we were going up into the haymow and they should be on standby. Once we were up there, we find it completely empty. We call Rob and tell him to go ahead and come in through the ramp door. Then he lets John know to come around and join us in the mow.

We take a good look around and don't even see any footprints in the dust.

"This whole farm looks like it's been deserted for the last two or three years," says the chief.

So we all head out to the barnyard.

"Well, Chief, we know this place is the right address. And it is or was owned by the Knowles family. We'll do some more investigating to see who is who. I'm sure that Jack Knowles lived here at some time. He has a driver's license with this address on it."

"Do you think we should go out back and see if there's anything back towards the pond? We could at least see if anyone's been driving through to get back there."

"Yes, let's go see if we can find any paths heading that way."

We all head out behind the garage and house. Back there we spread out and look for any paths to get through the woods. John calls out that he's found a dirt road behind the pole shed. So we all head over to him.

We follow the roadway for about half a mile before we come upon the pond. The roadway looks like it has had some use. The grass is flattened down where tires have driven on it. And back by the pond there is nothing to see. No buildings or vehicles to be seen.

It's a very pretty area. The setting is very calming. The pond is set in a flower-covered meadow. It would be the perfect place for a small cabin. The pond is decent sized. Probably about five acres in size.

We look around and find several piles of beer cans and empty booze bottles. The booze bottles are pretty much cheap whiskey and brandy brands. And looking a little closer there are several condoms strewn around the area.

"Well, Chief if looks like we found a private party spot probably for the local teenagers. It might pay to patrol the area once in a while."

"I agree with that, Duke. What do you think our next step should be in finding this Jake Knowles? He might be a big factor in your investigation."

"I'm guessing that Jack Knowles might be living in Madison. We'll check around here first. So chief we need to get those pictures from the tape and have all the officers on the force show them around. If he's in or around Black Crow we should be able to find him. We can also find out who owns this property as of now. If it's still in the family we can track who pays the taxes."

"I'm going to go call Joe Blaine. He's a special investigator on the Madison PD that was up here when they came to process the last murder scene. I'll give him a picture of this Jack Knowles. He can put out and APB for him down there. He said that he would give us any help he could."

"I'm also going to go talk to a guy named Jim Knowles. He was a golfing buddy with Ed Browning and three other guys. I talked to them the other day at the diner. I want to see if he's related to this Jack Knowles. Also, Rob, I need the contact you had with the safe company. I want to check something out that's been bugging me."

"What's bugging you, Duke?"

"I wonder how easy it is to crack one of their safes and how quickly it can be done. Somehow the thief got into those safes pretty quickly. There has to be some simple answer that we aren't seeing."

Everyone else headed back to the police station. Rob and I decided to stop at the register of deeds to see Markum Dooley. He can tell us who owns the house.

Once at the courthouse we go to the second floor. We go to the register of deeds office.

"Hello, Markum, good to see you again. We're here to check ownership of a property out on Mill Pond Road,"

"Hello, Duke, what's the address and I'll look it up for you?"

"It's 123 Mill Pond Road. There's no one living out there right now. In fact the whole place is falling apart from neglect."

"Well, Duke, let me grab my book and take a look. Here we are. That property was owned by Art Knowles. But the deed was transferred to Monroe County three years ago. The county took it because of unpaid taxes. I would think that they would eventually auction it off. I have no idea why they're sitting on it. I guess someone should bring it up at the next town council meeting."

"Well, thanks, Markum. It would be a nice piece of property to own. It's mostly wooded and pretty well secluded. I guess we'll check with the neighbors to get some history on the Knowles family. We're looking for a Jake Knowles. He shows that as his address on his driver's license. But he's definitely not living out there. Well, thanks, Markum, I'll catch you later."

"Rob, call the chief and tell him that the property is owned by the county now. Also tell him we're going to go out and talk to the neighbors out on Mill Pond Road. And ask him if he can find anyone that might have known the family. Someone had to have known them over the years."

We stop at the first place that's next to 123 Mill Pond Road. It's an old farmhouse, but has been kept up nicely. It's a nice pleasant light blue with white shutters. There's what looks like a new two-car garage next to the house. There's a car and pickup truck sitting in front of the garage.

We park and walk up to the front door. After knocking on the door, it's answered by a very pretty young woman. I introduce ourselves to her and she invites us to come in. She takes us down a long hallway to the back of the house where the kitchen is. It's a nice brightly lit room with what looks like extra windows added on two walls. She invites us to sit at the table and asks if we'd like anything to drink. We decline and let her know that we'd like to ask some questions about the farm next door.

She replies, "I'm Sara Johnson and my husband is George. He's asleep in the living room. He's been sick and is resting to hopefully get better. He has already missed two days of work and can't really afford to miss any more. But you don't want to hear about that. So what can I help you with?"

"It's nice to meet you, Mrs. Johnson. We're here checking on the people that used to live at the old farm down the road from you. We know a guy named Art Knowles used to own the place before he passed away. Did you or your husband ever know him or his family?"

"I'm afraid we haven't lived hear that long. We bought this place three years ago. As far as we know no one was living there since we've been here. At least we've never seen anyone. I wish I could be of more help."

"Did you or your husband live around here growing up?"

"No, we both moved here about four years ago when my husband got a job driving a log truck for the International Paper Mill. We came from Rockford, Illinois and had always wanted to live up here in the north woods. It's kind of our dream to be up here. I got a job in the office at the paper mill. I took a couple of vacation days to help George out. We have a daughter Jeanne and son Billy that are in school right now. So I guess you'd say were pretty new to the area."

"No problem. Mention it to your husband and if he knows anything let us know. You've done a nice job fixing the place up. I hope you enjoy living here."

"Thank you, we were hoping to raise a family here. We thought it would be a great place for the kids to grow up. There's the woods all around us, and the pond isn't too far behind us. There's plenty for kids to do and maybe learn something about nature at the same time."

"Well, good luck and we'll probably see you around town."

We left and drove down the road to the property on the other side of the Knowles place. There's a gravel driveway going back into the woods. We pulled in and didn't have to go for before we saw the house and barn. Both the house and barn are in just about as bad of shape as the Knowles place. The house is a little better as it isn't leaning at all. But it is in bad need of a coat of paint. The barn is leaning quite a bit, though. It has seen better days. I kind of wondered where any crops could have been planted. It seemed to be all wooded behind all these farms. I suppose the fields across the road belong to these farms. They must all be leased out or have been bought. All these farms have no decent farm machinery at them.

As we get out of our car, an older gent comes out of the house. He was bent at the waist and walked with a limp. Something you see in quite a few older men that have done a lot of physical work all their lives. He was dressed in bib coveralls that had seen a washing machine many a time.

I introduced Rob and myself to him. He said his name was Russ Finley and shook our hands. That confirmed my guess that he had done a lot of physical work. His hands were rough and heavily callused. And his knuckles were enlarged telling me he probably had arthritis.

"Mr. Finley, were asking around to see if anyone knew the Knowles family that lived down the road from you. We're looking for Jake Knowles. The name on the land deed was Art Knowles. Did you happen to know any of them?"

"Yes, I knew Art and the whole family. We used to help each other putting in and picking our crops. He bought that farm about the same time I bought this one. "That was forty years ago. He did have a son named Jake. That kid was a real piece of work."

"Art had nothing but trouble with that boy. He was lazy to start with. Art had trouble getting that kid to do any work around the place. And when he did get him to do any work it usually got screwed up."

"I do remember once instance when I was over there helping Art with partial demolition on the front of the barn. Jack had backed the feed truck into the siding putting a big hole in it. Art and I were going to strip part of the siding off to so he could replace it.

There was a basketball hoop mounted about ten feet up and needed to be removed. Art told Jack to take the hoop down while he and I went to the barn to get some pry bars and hammers so we could start the job."

"When we were walking back from the garage, we saw Jack had backed the truck up to the barn and was standing in the back with an axe. He then started to chop away at the barn around the basketball hoop."

Art hollered, "What the hell do you think you're doing?"

Jack just turned to us and said, "I'm taking the basketball hoop down like you told me."

"I think it was the smile on his face that pissed Art off the most. He told him to get a wrench out of the truck tool box and unbolt it."

"Jack was constantly getting kicked out of school. It was usually for fighting. And I guess his grades were terrible also."

"I'm surprised the woods round here didn't get burned down back then. Jack and his buddies would have bonfires going in the woods and sit around drinking beer and smoking dope."

"I swear the kid came over here and stole things from us. I couldn't prove it, but I would mention it to Art. Art always offered to pay, but I would decline. I could never prove any of it and they were not any better off than us."

"Jack finally left home when he was sixteen. We heard he was staying in Madison. But he usually came back home a few times a year. He'd be broke or in trouble with the law. I think he would steal money from Art and his wife Edith and then head back to Madison."

"Art didn't believe in banks but he got sick of Jack stealing what he had. There are only so many places to hide things. And Jack would have nothing else to do but hunt for it."

"Art finally decided it was safer to put his money in the bank than have Jack steal it. He would leave just enough lying around so Jack would find it and leave again."

"Art passed away about six or seven years ago. His wife Edith passed on a year before that. The way I heard it, Jack got the farm and then tried to sell it eventually. He had such a high price on it that no one would buy it. After he didn't pay the taxes for three years, the county took the place. I haven't seen or heard from Jack for at least four years. I would only guess that he's either in prison or maybe living in Madison. All I know is life got much better around here with him gone. I quit farming about five years ago and lease out the land to another farmer."

"Do you have any idea why the county hasn't auctioned off the farm yet? With the woods and pond at the back of the property, I would think it would be an easy sell."

"I've kind of wondered about that myself. It's been nice and quiet with no one living there. The fields across the road are prime farmland. It's being leased out to the same guy that I lease to."

"Do you remember the name of the realtor that was trying to sell the property for Jack?"

"Yea, I remember. It was Blackburn Realty out of Black River Falls. I believe they have or had an office in Black Crow."

"Okay, thanks for everything, Mr. Finley. If you think of anything else, give us a call at the Black Crow police station."

We get back in the car and Rob says, "That didn't seem to get us much."

"It gives us some leads to check out. He's using this address on his license so he probably sets some mail sent to him. We need to check with the post office to see where his mail gets forwarded to. Plus, the realty company had to have at least a phone number to get ahold of him. They should also have an address on their contract with him. Of course, he could have used a post office box to have the mail forwarded to."

"Plus, I'll get Madison PD working on looking for him there. So we at least have some areas to work on. It's the most we've had to work with so far. You never know where things will lead."

"Let's head back to the station and do some real investigating. I've got a good feeling about all this."

We get back to the station and the chief beckons us to his office. He asks if we found anything out.

I answered, "We talked to a Russ Finley that lives at the next farm. He remembers the Knowles family. Art and Edith farmed there and had one son, Jack. He was in trouble a lot in school and with the law. He took off from home when he was sixteen. They said he went to Madison."

"His folks are both deceased now and he had the house up for sale. Mr. Finley said he had too high a price on it, so it never sold. The taxes were not paid for three years, so the county took the farm. But for some reason the county hasn't auctioned it off yet."

"We've got a few things to check out. One is where does Jack get his mail. He has the Mill Pond address on his driver's license. So we'll see where his mail gets forwarded to."

"I also want to check the realtor that had the contract to sell the farm. Blackburn Realty is supposed to have an office here in town. They would have to have had some contact information to get ahold of Jack if they had any offers on the place."

"Yes, there is a Blackburn Realty office over on Elm Street. It's only one block from here," replies the chief. "So, why don't you and Rob get started working on those leads. I've been asking around to see if anyone knew Jack. So far no one remembers him. It seems hard to believe that someone that was that much trouble wouldn't be remembered. But I'll keep asking around."

"Rob, which lead do you want to take? You'd probably be better checking out the mail end. I'm not that savvy on the computer. I'm going to call Joe Blaine in Madison first."

"Okay, Duke, I'll take the post office. Are you going to call the realtor or go see them?"

"I might drive over there as soon as I find where their office is in town. I'll let you know when I'm ready if you'd like to ride along."

"Sounds good, Duke, I'll get to work on my end right now."

"Also, Rob, can you give me the phone number for your contact at Gardall safe. I want to get a call into them yet today."

I went to the desk I was using and got the phone number for Joe Blaine at the Madison PD. I dialed and got the head desk at the police station. I asked for Joe Blaine. The woman that answered told me to hold while she transferred the call.

The next thing I heard was, "Hey, Duke, it's good to hear from you so soon. Did you catch your killer yet? I figured it would be in the news if you had. I'm guessing you need something from me."

"That's a good guess, Joe, I actually do need some help. We've got a suspect we're looking for. We think he might be living somewhere in Madison. That's where he moved to years ago. He pawned a piece of jewelry from one of the thefts in Madison. The address on his license was for here in Black Crow, but it's a deserted farm now."

"I'd like to send you a picture of him. We got it off a recording of him pawning the necklace. We're doing all we can to see if he's still around here. Can you spare a little time to see if he can be found in Madison?"

"We'd be glad to help out, Duke. Do you have a name? That way I can get started checking in the computer."

"Sounds good Joe, his name is Jack Knowles. He looks pretty scruffy in the picture, but he might have cleaned himself up since then. He did get four hundred dollars for the necklace. Who knows if he used it for drugs or decided to clean himself up a little."

"We're also checking to see what mailing address he's using. I'm checking with the realtor that he had his farm up for sale with. They had to have an address or phone number to get ahold of him when needed."

"We're also trying to check with the post office to see where his mail is being forwarded to. We should have some answers by tomorrow. It's getting kind of late today so we might have to wait until tomorrow on some of this."

"I'll fax his picture to you as soon as we get it printed from the recording. I'll need your fax number."

"Okay, Duke, I'll be waiting for the picture while checking out the name. I'll probably check back with you tomorrow to compare our findings."

"Okay, Joe, I'll talk to you then."

Something had been tickling me in the back of my brain. It was like a light bulb suddenly went off in my head. I had heard the Knowles name somewhere else and I just remembered where. I interviewed the four old-timers that meet at the diner every week. I forgot to check and see if Jim Knowles is related to Art and Jack Knowles. It's getting close to suppertime, so I'd better get some calls made.

I decide to see if the realty business is still in Black Crow. I grab a phone book and look under realtors. There I find Blackburn Realty right away and see their address is on Oak Street.

That's just a couple of blocks away on the edge of the town square. I decide to call instead of running over there. I grab the phone and dial their number. Someone answers on the third ring.

A woman answers and tells me her name is Mary. I tell her my name and that I'm working with the police department. She then asks how she can be of service to me.

I reply, "Mary, I understand your agency had a property up for sale around three or four years ago. The address is 123 Mill Pond Road outside of town here. We're trying to get in touch with the person that owned it then. His name is Jack Knowles. Is it possible for you to access any information about him?"

"Hold on a minute, Mr. Moran, I wasn't here then, but I'll look in our records and see what I can find. Why don't I give you a call back? I might have to dig through the files if it's not in the computer."

"That works for me, Mary. Call me back at 207-8115. I'll be here for a while yet."

Rob was on the phone at the desk next to me. I heard him thank whoever he was talking to and hang up the phone.

"Rob, did you find out anything about Jack's jobs through Social Security?"

"They informed me that he hasn't had anything put in a Social Security account because he doesn't have an account. At least not under that name. Apparently, he's never had a job that put money into Social Security for him. So that's a dead end. Did you find anything from the realty outfit?"

"I'm waiting for a call back from them right now. Do you have a phone number for that safe manufacturing company? I want to ask them a question."

Just as Rob gave me the phone number and name of his contact my phone started to ring. So I grabbed it and announced myself.

"Mr. Moran, it's Mary from Blackburn Realty. I've found the contract for that property we tried to sell. Apparently, it didn't sell and the contract didn't get extended. The contract was with a Jack Knowles. It doesn't show an address for him, but there is a phone number. It's 608-266-1267. Is there anything else you'd like to know?"

"Just out of my curiosity, how much was the farm listed for?"

"It was listed for 150,000 dollars. Its ninety-five acres, but the house and barn were in bad shape, according to the notes we have here. It was listed as two parcels. There's five acres where the house and barn are located. Then there are ninety acres across the road that are tillable."

"Well, thanks a lot, Mary. I appreciate all the help you gave me. Have a nice day, and if I need a realtor, I'll give you a call."

"Well, Rob here's a phone number. Can you get on the computer and run a reverse check on it? We know the number and his name so maybe we can get an address from his provider."

"I'll get on it right now. Let's see what we have here. That number is from one of those prepaid cell phones. It's from quite a while ago, and there's no way to track anything from them. There's also no way to do a phone tap on them either. I'm afraid we're at a dead end there. You could call the number, but I think that would just alert him that we're looking for him."

"You might be right, Rob, but I'm going to try it anyways. I'll just ask for George and see what he says."

I dial the phone number, and I immediately get a recording telling me the number is no longer in use.

"Well, Rob, that number isn't good anymore. Is it too late, you think, to try the post office?"

"Yes, its six o'clock, and I think the people we need to talk to would probably be gone now. I'll try first thing in the morning."

"Let's go get a bite to eat. I'm starving and we need a break to figure out what all we need to do next. Let's go to the diner to eat unless you have a date, Rob. I'll even buy. I want to come back and make some more calls before calling it a day."

"I have no date and will let you buy supper. Don't worry, though, I won't eat as much as I did at that buffet lunch."

After a great meal of homemade meatloaf at the diner, we got back to the station. I thought I'd call the Gardall Safe Company on the chance there might be someone that could answer my questions. I dialed the number Rob gave me and got a canned recording stating their working hours. I'll have to wait until eight thirty in the morning to call back.

My next thing to do was find a number for Jim Knowles. I checked the local phone book, which covered our whole county. I found a listing for Jim Knowles with an address of 618 Pine Street in Chaney. So, I went ahead and dialed his phone number. After a few rings there was an answer.

They answered with a simple hello and nothing else.

I relied, "Hello this is Duke Moran with the Black Crow police department. Is this the Knowles residence?"

The lady replied, "Yes, it is. This is Judy Knowles. Who would you like to speak with?"

"I'm looking for Jim Knowles. I spoke with him the other day at Barb's Diner."

"Yes, Jim is my husband. If you hold, I'll get him for you. He's in the basement working on one of his models."

A few minutes later a man's voice comes on the phone. "Hello this is Jim. Who am I speaking with?"

"Hello, Mr. Knowles this is Duke Moran from the Black Crow police department. We talked the other day at the Barb's Diner. I'm investigating the Browning and Anderson murders."

"Yes, I remember you. What can I do for you today?"

"I'm calling to see if you are related in any way to the Knowles family that used to live out on Mill Pond Road?"

"Yes, I am. That was my brother Art and his wife Edith. They also had a son Jack. Both Art and Edith are gone now, and I haven't heard a thing about Jack for years."

"Were actually trying to get a lead on where the son, Jack, is at. We were informed that he might have moved to Madison. Do you know if there are any other relatives or maybe friends he might have living there?"

"I know of no one in Madison that's related to us. And I have no idea who his friends might be. We avoided Jack as much as we could. He caused Art and Edith all kinds of heartache. Jack was constantly getting into trouble and stealing from his parents on a regular basis."

"I wish I could help you more but as I said, we haven't heard anything about Jack in years. I know he tried to sell the house and ended up losing that. I wish you luck in finding him."

"Well, thanks, Mr. Knowles for your time. Maybe we'll see you around at the diner some time."

"Well, Rob, I'm going to call it a night. I think I'll stop and see if Jane wants to go for ice cream or maybe something a little stronger. I'm hoping tomorrow is more fruitful for us. I don't believe our culprit is going to stop at these two burglaries."

I stopped by Jane's apartment to see if she was at home. I'm in luck. She's sitting out on her little deck that's attached to her apartment. Of course, she looks fantastic as usual. Jane gets up out of her lounge chair and gives me a big hug and kiss.

She replies, "This is a pleasant surprise. I was just thinking about you. Maybe I have ESP."

"Have you eaten yet? I might have something I can heat up for you. Or we could start with dessert." This came a big juicy kiss and her pelvis rubbing against me.

I was trying to come up with a smart answer, but I seemed to be tongue-tied. So I just picked her up and slid open the door and took her to the bedroom. Where I tried to throw her on the bed, but she didn't let go and we both tumbled onto the mattress.

She said, "Before we do anything, we're hitting the shower. I want to be nice and fresh for you."

"I don't believe it, there is a heaven. It might take me awhile to get you clean. I hate to miss any spots."

"Okay, big guy, get in there and get the water running. At least we'll be saving water showering together. And we can't waste a lot of time. I have to get up early for work. You have a habit of wearing a girl out."

Between the shower and what happened afterward took us to about midnight. Jane then kicked me out, so she could get some sleep. I managed to drive home without incident. We even forgot about eating. No wonder my stomach is growling.

I pulled up to my garage and headed for the back door. I walked into the porch and heard and felt crunching under my feet. I know right away that it's broken glass. This is getting old quickly.

I pulled my gun right away and tried the door. It was unlocked so I slowly opened it. The house was dead silent and completely dark. My first thought was there was another burglary and killing just like the others.

I went into the kitchen and grabbed a flashlight. Then I headed for the basement to get the electricity back on. I made it to the back of the basement where the fuse box is located and pushed the lever up to turn everything back on. I had to go back up the stairs to turn on the lights. Now I had some light to see by.

There was no one in the basement so I went upstairs and went through the rest of the house. I found no one and everything seemed to be in its place.

I headed for the basement to check out the hidden room. It was still closed up just as before. I slid the shelving out of the way and opened the wood door. I didn't know what to expect.

I hit the light switch for the room and noticed something missing right away.

All the cash was gone. The table in the center of the room was bare. But I noticed that the jewelry all seemed to be there on the shelf where we found it. The body was also still in the corner.

I immediately called Rob and told him to get ahold of the chief. I let him know about the missing money. My next thing to do was check the laptop to see what the camera picked up.

When I got upstairs, I fired up the computer. I opened the program for the hidden camera and hit Play.

It showed a figure coming in the door. They had a sweatshirt with a hood pulled over their head. They kept their face hidden from the camera. There was nothing that stood out to determine if it was a man or a woman. They also had gloves on so I couldn't even tell what race they might be.

At this time, I heard a couple of cars come into the driveway. I went to the back door to let them in.

It was the chief and Rob. I told them to come in and look at the laptop first. I replayed it for them from the beginning.

The chief's first words were that the person had to know about the camera. The way he was dressed and that he knew to not look up. And on his way out, all you could see was the back of his head.

The intruder then took a bar of some sort and broke the glass out into the porch. Next thing it showed was the person leaving.

The chief said, "Somehow the suspect had to know about the camera. Only a few of us knew about it. There was the three of us and my son Rick that put in in. I don't think any of us told anyone. So I will be talking to Rick, and there will be hell to pay if he told someone."

"Chief, I take it there hasn't been any calls about any burglary's so far? Hopefully there will be none."

"No, Duke, I haven't been informed about anything serious happening tonight. I'll call in just to be sure, though. Let's have a look at the room in the basement."

"I'm going to close up this room and hit the hay. Tomorrows bound to be a long day. I'll see the both of you tomorrow."

Chapter 23

* * * * * * * * * *

Friday June 28

After a restless night of trying to sleep, the sun woke me up at eight o'clock. It was shining through my window right in my face. So it was either I had to get up and close the curtains or get up and stay up.

Now that I'm up, I could really use a cup of coffee. I need to buy one of those coffee machines that you can get ready the night before. So then when you wake up the coffee would be ready.

I grabbed a quick shower and headed for the diner for that much-needed coffee and a bite to eat. While eating I remember that I didn't even clean up the glass by the back door. Much less fix it. It would have to wait. I doubted the killer would be back for more stuff. Especially during the daytime when he could be easily spotted.

I get to the station and find Rob on the telephone. I'm guessing it's probably with the post office.

It's past eight thirty, so I figure it's a good time to call the safe company up. I dial the number Rob had given me and wait for an answer.

I finally get an answer with a sweet, "Hello, how may I help you."

I answer, "I'm calling from Black Crow, Wisconsin. I'm with the police department here, and I need some information on safe cracking."

"We don't normally give out information like that to just anyone. We would need proof as to who you are. Why don't you hold for a minute and I'll put you through to my manager?"

She abruptly puts me on hold to listen to some canned Reggae music. I'm just getting into the song that's playing when it's interrupted by a man's voice.

"Hello, this is George Kaplan of the Gardall Safe Company. How may I be of assistance to you."

"Hello, my name is Duke Moran. I'm calling from the Black Crow police department in Wisconsin. I have a couple of questions I'd like to ask you."

"Sure, always glad to help out our law enforcement folks whenever I can. What would you like to know?"

"My question is about your model 18FL48U floor safe. How hard is it to break into one of these without having to damage it? And how quickly can it be done?"

"With practice and some knowledge about safecracking it's not rocket science. All you need is a good stethoscope. If a person has one of the safes, they just need to practice learning the sounds of the tumblers dropping. The safe combination can be changed from the inside once open. Then with practice you learn the sounds of the different tumblers dropping. Once you are used to the sounds, it can be done very quickly. Is this what you needed to know?"

"Yes, it is, we've had two of these safes emptied out, and I'm trying to figure how it could be done. So I think you might have just supplied the way it was probably done."

"If you can find out how many of these safes were sold in your area it would probably help point to the culprit. I can look and see how many were sold to the various supply houses in Wisconsin. Do you have any idea of the dates we could start with?

"I know that three of the safes we have found were installed in 1985. We checked with a supplier in Madison that had bought four of that safe from you. I guess we need to find out what happened to that fourth one."

"I'm looking in the computer right now and I found that record. That safe wasn't a big seller because of the work involved to install them. I only show the four of them going to Wisconsin that year. I show none the year before and the same for the year after. A person could learn to open safes on a different model. Most are similar in their makeup. But using the same model would definitely make it easier to learn."

"Well, thanks, Mr. Kaplan for your help. I think I'll get ahold of Mecca Security to see where that other safe went."

"Okay, Mr. Moran, give me a call if you need any further assistance."

"Well, Rob, I think we know how the safes were broken into. All it takes is a stethoscope and some practice to learn how to open a safe. We need to find out where that fourth safe from Gardall to Mecca Security was sold."

"I also hope we hear something from Joe Blaine in Madison about the location of Jack Knowles. No one from our area has called in about him in this area.

"I'm going to call Mecca Security now and see if I can track down that fourth safe."

I find the number for Mecca and dial it up. After a few rings, I get an answer. I then hear, "This is Mecca Security, how may I help you?"

"Hello, I need to talk to someone about some safe sales from back in 1985. I'm calling from Black Crow police department which is north east of you. My partner talked to someone earlier, but I don't have a name."

"It was probably Mr. Jones in our sales office. If you'll hold, I'll transfer you to him."

I get put on hold for about two minutes before I get a voice again.

"Hello, this is John Jones. How can I be of assistance to you?"

"Hello, John, I'm calling from the Black Crow police department. I believe you talked to my partner about a week ago."

"Yes, I did. Do you have more questions that need our assistance?"

"Yes, you told Rob there were three safes sold to a Bobby Brooks here in Black Crow. The people at Gardall Safe told me that there were four safes sent to you back then. Would you happen to know who received the fourth safe?"

"Well, let me take a look here at our records. Luckily, we have everything on computer so it should be quick. Here we go. That fourth safe was sold and shipped to a Chad Reardon in Black River Falls. I have an address here if you'd like it. Hopefully it's still good."

"Yes, John, I would really appreciate it. We're getting desperate for leads in our case."

"The address is 879 Fourth Street in Black River Falls. The buyer's name was Chad Reardon. Is there anything else I can help you with, Mr. Moran?"

"No, that is great, John. You've been a great help to us and we really appreciate it. So enjoy the rest of your day."

"The same to you, Mr. Moran, thanks for calling."

"Well, Rob we have a name for the fourth safe. I think we might need to take a trip to Black River and check this out. We have a name and address to check out. I'll see if we can find a phone number to call first."

"Duke, do you really think this Jack Knowles could be our murderer? He doesn't seem smart enough to pull something like this off. Plus, I think we'd have seen someone that looks like him around here. He would stand out like a sore thumb around here. He looks like a mountain man or grizzly bear."

"I agree with you, Rob. But he had to get that jewelry from somewhere. I think he either knows our suspect or came into contact with him somehow."

"I've found a phone number for this Chad Reardon in Black River. I'm going to call it now."

I dial the number and have a short wait. I get a recording informing me that the number has been disconnected.

"Well, Rob, it looks like we need to run into Black River and check out this house. If we leave now, we can have lunch over there and be back fairly early this afternoon."

"I'm game; let's hit the road. I'll let the chief know where we're going and why. Do you want to make sure the car is gassed up and ready to go?

"I'm on it, Rob. See if we have a map of Black River anywhere. It could save us some time."

We get on the road and make it to Black River in less than an hour. Rob has found our street and gives me directions to get there. We pull up in front of an old Victorian house. It's a beautiful house that's been kept in mint condition. From the peak all the way down both eaves there is carved, very fancy lattice work. The house is basically white with green and gold trim. You wouldn't think those colors would work, but they were put in just the right places. It's something you have to see to appreciate.

We get out of our car and walk up to the front door. There is a wraparound porch going around three sides of the house. There are beautiful hardwood rockers lined up across the front porch section.

I ring the doorbell, and we hear someone coming to the door. We can also see them because the door is three quarters glass. The person that answers the door is an elderly lady that looks like she could be someone's grandmother.

"Hello, I'm Duke Moran and this is Detective Turner. We're from the Black Crow police department. Is this the Chad Reardon residence?"

"No, I'm afraid it's not, at least not anymore. We bought the house three years ago from the Reardon family. The way I understand it is that Mrs.

Reardon passed away about four years ago. Then Mr. Reardon passed away a few days after her. The stories I've heard is that he died of a broken heart. They had been married for over forty years."

"We're checking out the sale of some home safes from the 1980s. Mr. Reardon had purchased one back then and we're checking to see if he still has it. It would be a floor safe."

"We have no safe in this house. I think we would have noticed if there was one. I believe the family had an estate sale after their folks passed on. I do know that one son lives here in town. I can check the phone book if you want. If he's in there, then so would be his address."

"That would be great. I don't think we caught your name."

"I'm Jane Jones and my husband is Jim. He's at the barbershop getting a haircut right now."

"I've found the son's name here in the phone book. His name is George Reardon and he lives at 414 North Highland Street. That's on the other side of town. If you go back down to Main Street and take a right. You go through a couple of street lights and you'll find Highland almost at the edge of town. North Highland would be to the left."

"Well, thank you, Mrs. Jones and have a pleasant rest of your day."

So Rob and I head over to Highland thinking it's probably a waste of time. There's no telling what could have happened to that safe over the years.

We arrive at our destination to find it's in a newer part of the city. The homes are a cut above your normal ranch house. They're sort of like mini mansions. Decent in size, but not overly huge. All the lawns are beautifully manicured and houses built of mostly brick. The whole area seems out of place for being in the north woods.

The house we needed had a circular driveway. We pulled into the driveway and parked behind what looked like a brand-new Audi. I'm not saying I couldn't afford one but that would stand out like a sore thumb in Black Crow.

The house was a light-colored beige brick. It, of course, had the normal two-story pillars across the front. I'm sure that in this neighborhood it's called a veranda.

We walked up to the front door, which was a massive double door made of carved wood. We rang the doorbell and heard it play some classical song. Something like Beethoven or Mozart.

I don't know if someone was watching or what but the door opened immediately. It was an elderly lady in a maid's uniform.

She asked, "May I help you?"

I replied, "Yes we're from the Black Crow police department. We were informed that George Reardon lives here. We have some questions we'd like to ask him. Does he happen to be home?

"Yes, Mr. Reardon happened to come home to check on his wife. She has been ill lately. Why don't you wait here, and I'll see if Mr. Reardon will see you?"

She closed the door on us and we were left standing there. Rob decided to step down and check out the Audi. I joined him and we walked around the car to look at the fine German engineering.

All of a sudden there was a man standing in the front doorway calling to us. So we went back up the stairs to talk to him.

He didn't invite us in. He just stood there while I introduced us. He asked why we were interested in his old homestead.

I said, "We're investigating some murder/burglaries that happened in Black Crow. We're checking out people that bought a certain floor safe back in the 1980s. The name Chad Reardon was one of the names we received that bought one. I believe he was your father. The lady that lives in your old house claims there is no floor safe in there."

"No, there never was a safe in the house that I know of. But I do remember my dad buying one. He just never got around to installing it."

"We had an estate sale after my mother and dad passed on. I remember a guy buying it because he asked to borrow a two wheeled cart to haul the safe to his vehicle."

"Do you remember the vehicle or anything about the man at all? And did he write a check maybe?"

"I'm not sure on the vehicle. I think it was light colored. All I saw was the rear end of it, and he loaded it into the back end. It was either a pickup truck or van. I wasn't paying a lot of attention because people were asking me questions about other things. I just wanted to make sure he brought the cart back."

"As far as the man himself, I don't remember much about him. The only reason I remember anything is because the safe was an odd item to see at a sale. You don't see floor safes that much. It's kind of a specialty item. Anyways all I remember about the guy is he was around my age, about the same build, and was wearing a service type shirt. I didn't pay too much attention to what insignia was on it. I do remember that something was eerie about it. I'm pretty sure he paid cash for the safe. That's about all I can remember. Sorry."

"That's fine. It's more than we had before. Thank you for your time, and I hope your wife gets better. Also, that's a great-looking car you have there."

"Thanks; I just got it. And my wife is doing better today. Thanks for your concern. I wish you luck on your investigation."

Back in the car, I asked Rob if he was hungry. I realized that was a dumb question once it left my lips. Rob is always hungry. I figured I'd try to find a normal restaurant to hopefully curb how much he would eat. I didn't want to spend all day watching him eat.

We made it back to Black Crow around two o'clock. We headed right to the station to check in with the chief. We entered his office to find him on the phone. He finished his call and told us that was a Jake Flowers calling to say his house got broken into last night.

"Isn't that someone you two interviewed? The name sounded familiar when the dispatcher told me about it. So, I called him to personally check it out. He told me the two of you had been there to talk to him about a safe he had installed years ago. Maybe the two of you should go talk to him again. I did send a patrol car there to make out a report."

"Okay, Chief, we'll head right over there. Also, Chief, do you have any idea how the suspect knew we had a camera hidden in my house? The only ones that should have known about it were you, me, Rob, and your son Rick. I'm sure the three of us didn't tell anyone."

"I'm sure the three of us didn't say anything. I didn't see Rick this morning when I got up. I think he was still in bed. But I'm going to go hunt him down now. He's the only person that could have leaked anything."

Rob and I headed out to interview Jake Flowers. When we arrived to his house, we saw the squad car was still there. We headed up to the door and rang the bell. Mr. Flowers answered the door and let us in. Officer John Dole was sitting at the dining room table with his note pad in front of him. We all said hello, and John said he was about done with his report.

"Mr. Flowers can you rehash what you just told Officer Dole here. I hate to make you repeat it, but it would be better to repeat it in case you missed something."

"Okay, my wife and I went down to Madison yesterday to take in a comedy act at the old Belfore Theater. We had decided to stay overnight and had a reservation at the Holiday Inn on the beltline."

"We got back here about one o'clock. We stayed in Madison for the morning to do some shopping. We came in the back door and found the glass broken in it. And the wood door was unlocked. I remember locking it when we left. We entered the house and looked around for any damage and didn't see any. Everything seemed in order until we went upstairs to unpack."

"When I went into the closet to stow away the suitcases, I noticed the floor safe was open. It was empty when I looked in, and there were our papers strewn about the room. So I immediately called the police station."

"Officer Dole why don't you call in and see if they can get someone out here to check for fingerprints."

"What all did you have in the safe, Mr. Flowers? I know you told us that you didn't keep much money in it."

"No, there wasn't much money in there. In fact, before we left, I went in there to get some cash for our trip. There was exactly twelve hundred dollars left in there. I'm just glad that we were not at home when it happened. We might be in the same shape as those other two couples ended up."

"Well, thank you, Mr. Flowers. Officer Dole will stay here until the fingerprint guy gets here. If you think of anything else, please give us a call."

Rob and I head back to the station house. When we get back, we go directly to the chief's office. He motions us in and tells us to have a seat.

"Well, did you guys find out anything from the break-in? Is it the same MO as the other break-ins?"

"Everything is the same except there were no killings luckily. The glass in the back door was broken outwards and the safe opened up without force. There was twelve hundred dollars in the safe that was taken."

"The only other difference is that the electricity wasn't turned off. My guess is that it's the same person and he either didn't know the Flowers were gone for the night. Or he was just playing it safe and wanting it to be a quick heist."

"What I don't understand is why the person is only robbing where he knows who has that particular type safe. That's the only common denominator in all the burglaries. The robber had to also know all the people somehow. I think he had to be at all their houses at some time."

"You're right, Duke and I did talk to my son Rick today. He says that he can only think of one person that he might have told about the camera. And that is our very own daytime dispatcher Carmon."

"As you know she likes to party with different men quite frequently. My son Rick is one of them. He was trying to impress her with how smart he is with electronics. I guess one night he hooked up her new sound system for her television. They had been drinking, of course, and he thinks he might have bragged how he set up the surveillance system in your house, Duke."

"So, I think we need to get Carmon in here and question her about it."

"Rob, why don't you go out and ask Carmon to come in here. I see Tom is out there. Have him take over the dispatcher desk while we question her."

Rob came in with Carmon in just a few minutes. You could tell she was nervous and even a little scared. We had decided that the chief would start out the questioning, since he was her boss and she was used to being around him a lot.

"Have a seat, Carmon. I think you know Rob and Duke here. I've asked you to come in here so we can clear something up. I've talked to my son Rick and he told me the two of you have gone out a few times."

"Now I have a few questions for you. You're not in trouble, but I need some information I hope you can give me. Rick says he might have mentioned to you about installing a camera in Duke's house. Do you recall him saying anything about that?"

"Yes, I do remember him telling me that. I had asked him where he was that day. I wanted to go to an art show in Black River and he had promised to take me. When he canceled our trip, he wouldn't tell me why. Then that night he told me he had a job to do. Of course, I didn't believe him because I've caught him lying to me before."

"He was all hot and bothered and wanted to go to my place for... you know what. He can be very enticing when he wants something. But I held my ground and threatened to break up with him. He then said if I could keep a secret, he'd tell me. I as much as accused him of being with another women."

"Well, he said the job he had was a big secret. He had to install a hidden camera in a house for the police. He told me it was for the newest member of the police force."

"Everybody in town knows who that is. Anyways I forgave Rick and agreed to go to my place. I never told a soul about it. I know with working here that whatever I hear in here stays in here."

"Where were you when the two of you were talking about this?"

"We were in the diner having some pie and coffee. There weren't that many people in there."

"Do you recall any of the people near you?"

"I do remember that Nick Anders and his wife were in the next booth. They were alone because their kids would have been in school. And I remember Eddy Jones and John Jones sitting at the bar counter talking. I don't recall anyone else."

"Do you know if they overheard you at all?"

"I really don't know. I might have gotten a little loud when I was mad. Nobody seemed to pay any attention to us. I hope I didn't cause any problems."

"No, don't worry about it. Nobody got hurt, but Rick should know to keep his mouth shut. You can go back to work. Thanks for helping us out."

"Well, Chief, I'm going to go call Joe Blaine in Madison to see where he is with finding Jack Knowles."

I went to the desk I've been using to call Joe. As I sat down to find the phone number, Carmon calls over to me that I have a phone call. She transfers it to my phone and I answer it.

"Hello, this is Duke Moran, what can I do for you?"

"Hello, Duke it's Joe Blaine from Madison. How are you doing up there in God's country?"

"We're getting by, Joe. I was just going to call you. We keep hitting dead ends up here. So I thought I'd check to see if you found any more out about our Jack Knowles."

"That's why I'm calling. We found Knowles this morning. But I'm afraid it's not good news. He's been murdered. Someone took a knife to him. He had four stab wounds in his chest. It's a pretty bloody mess. It looks like he put up a fight. There were some cuts on his hands where he tried to block his attacker."

"It happened in an old abandoned warehouse. The buildings are all pretty old in that area and a lot are actually falling down. We wouldn't have found his body but a patrol car saw a van come out of the area early this morning. It sparked their interest because you never see traffic in that area especially in the early morning."

"So they drove through the area and saw a garage door hanging open. They checked the area out on a regular basis and know that door is always shut. So they went in to check it out. They saw the body as soon as their headlights lit up the interior of the building. They called it in but didn't have much of a description on the van. It was too far away when they saw it. All they got was that it was light colored."

"The crime scene investigators say there's not much evidence to check out. The building is empty and the killing took place just inside the door. It looks like the killer took Knowles to the warehouse and got him out of the vehicle and stabbed him right there. There was no one we could find around that area that could have seen anything. Then he just drove off, and it's just by chance that the officers saw the vehicle."

"We'll do some investigating, which will be just asking questions of our various contacts. I think it's going to be tough to find where he was staying unless someone reports him missing. He seemed to be living under the radar as it was. So about all I can do is let you know if we find anything."

"Well, that's a bummer, Joe. I do see your dilemma, though. It's like looking for a needle in a haystack. We appreciate all your help and I'll keep in touch."

I grabbed Rob and we went back into the chief's office. I informed them both of what I'd just learned.

"So it looks like Jack Knowles is a dead end. We'll probably never know how he got that necklace. I don't like him for the murders, though. Someone would have noticed him around the area. I have someone in mind that I think we should bring in for questioning. It might be a long shot but a lot of evidence seems to point to one person possibly."

"Who do you have in mind, Duke?"

"I think we should talk to John Jones. He has a white van and wears shirts with a service emblem on it for his rodent business. He also has history with my house. There's a good chance he might have known about the hidden room. He also questions me about the crimes every time I see him. Of course, he is the mayor and could just be concerned about the town's safety."

"I don't know what could have triggered him to do these things after all these years, though. I've known him most of my life and he is a little odd but seems pretty normal."

"He also has had the perfect opportunity to be in the victims' homes. He could also know them both socially and professionally."

"I think I'll run home and get that laptop computer that Rick hooked up to that camera. I'll bring it here to the station so we can hook it up to the bigger screen computer we have. That way maybe we can pick out something about the intruder. Maybe his mannerisms or the shape of his body will stand out. The laptop screen is pretty small and harder to see."

"I'll be back in about half an hour. Rob, can you go pick us up some sandwiches from the diner? I'm starving and it's already six thirty. See you guys shortly."

I get home and run in the back door. I unlock the back door and walk into the kitchen. The first thing I notice is the basement door hanging open. As I take a step in that direction, I feel the presence of someone behind me. The next thing I feel is a stabbing pain in my back.

I automatically make a fist with my left hand and swing it low and behind me. We were taught that in Army. Every day they would make us practice it. Anyways I swung my fist up into the person's privates. I was hoping that it was a male. This wouldn't work with a woman.

I connected with his baby maker and heard the breath getting knocked out of him. At the same time, I turned and as the guy bent over forwards in definite pain. I brought my knee up right into his head as he fell forward.

The force of his head coming down and my knee coming up into him knocked him backwards. At the same time, I felt myself blacking out and my legs giving out. I don't remember hitting the floor.

Chapter 24

. . . .

Saturday June 24

I wake up, and it's so bright I have a hard time keeping my eyes open. I hope if I'm dead that this is heaven. There's a lot of bright color all around me. I see a face above me, and it's surrounded by a bright light. I can tell she's a female and very pretty. Then I see another bright face next to the first one and just as pretty. The second one looks familiar, and I strain to see her better.

Finally, the brightness seems to gradually go away, and I recognize Jane. The other woman is dressed all in white. There are flowers all around me like I'm lying in a flower garden. I ask, "Did something happen to you, Jane? Are we in heaven?"

Then the Jane figure said, "I see the drugs are working for you. I'm afraid you're not in heaven, lover boy. I'm afraid you're just in the hospital and this is nurse Nan."

"So what happened to me? I remember getting home and someone apparently attacked me. I don't remember anything after that."

"Well, you caught the killer after he tried to kill you. It had to be the weirdest capture in history. I'll let the chief explain it to you. He's just outside in the waiting room. Maybe Nan will go get him for you."

"I'll be glad to go fetch him for you. I'll take my time so you two can have some time alone. Just take it easy on him, Jane. They said the knife wound was pretty deep. The pain meds are doing their job right now, but we don't want that wound to open back up."

A few minutes later, Chief Turner and Rob both come into the room. They both had big smiles on their faces. Of course, the first thing they ask is how I'm feeling.

"You both look like you've caught a mouse. I'm glad to see someone's happy to see me laid up in bed. I'm feeling pretty good considering the alternative. Is someone going to tell me what happened? All I remember is walking into my kitchen and getting a stabbing pain in my back. I think I got a couple of hits into whoever attacked me. Then I must have blacked out."

"Well, it looks like you were attacked from behind and managed to lay out your attacker. Then you must have blacked out and fell on top of him. Apparently, you managed to knock him out, and he stayed that way with you lying on top of him. Did you get a look at him at all?"

"I didn't get a look at him because it all happened so fast. I do remember bringing a fist back into his crotch. Then I turned as he was falling toward me and I brought my knee up into his head. That's all I can remember."

"You must have a hard knee because it gave him a concussion and he was pretty groggy when Rob found you laying on him. Rob ran to your house when you didn't come back to the station. Who knows what could have happened if we weren't expecting you back? Do you have any clue as to who attacked you?"

"I know it sounds corny, but I had an odd feeling it could be John Jones. That's why I wanted to look at the laptop again. I thought maybe if we watched it closely, we could pick up some habits he had. So who was it that attacked me? I'm guessing it's the same person we've been looking for."

"You guessed it right. It was our beloved mayor Mr. Jones. We took him to the hospital after we got you pulled off of him. He was somewhat conscious when Rob got there."

"Yeah, Duke, he was trying to get out from beneath you. You had him pinned in the doorway, and he didn't have the strength or leverage to move you. His arms were pinned between the two of you."

"I actually left you on top of him until the paramedics got there. I didn't want to move you and risk further injury to you. The paramedics actually left the knife stuck in you and transported you that way. They said it probably saved your life leaving it in you. It helped plug the wound and kept you from bleeding out."

"Has JJ admitted to the crimes? And have you done a search of his home yet? We're going to need evidence to get him convicted of the other crimes."

"He hasn't admitted to anything yet. He won't even talk to us and he law-yered up right away. The only thing he said right away was that you attacked him. When we asked why he was in your house he tried to tell us you asked him to treat your place for rodents. He must have figured you would die from the knife wound."

"We do have some proof he knows about the hidden room. You must have moved the camera in your house. When we retrieved the laptop and fired it up, we got a surprise. It showed Jones going into the hidden room. He must have gone in there while waiting for you to come home. When we went down to check the room out some of the jewelry seemed to be missing. We did find it in his pockets."

"We have a search warrant coming this morning so we can do a search of Jones's house. Hopefully we can find some of the cash there. Luckily Rob wrote down the serial numbers on all of it. As soon as I get the call that we have the warrant, we'll be heading over there."

"I'm glad you're going to be all right. Everybody we meet in town has been asking about you. I'm sure you'll be getting a hero's welcome when you get out of here. A lot of people are relieved to have the killer behind bars. Now it's up to us to make sure we have a tight case against him."

All of a sudden, a man with a white coat walks in the room. He introduces himself as Dr. Thompson.

"So how's our hero patient doing? Let me just check your vitals out quickly."

After checking my heart and pulse, he marks it in my chart. He then says, "You're doing really great for a man near death yesterday. It's going to take a while to get your strength back, though. You lost quite a lot of blood."

"So how soon can I get out of here? I've got things to do, and I hate lying around doing nothing."

"I'm afraid you're going to be with us for a while. With the blood you lost and the depth of that cut you're still not out of the woods yet. Moving around could break things loose inside. We'll get you on your feet today but just to stand for a moment. Then maybe tonight you can take a few steps. I'm not going to let you undo all the work I did on you. I'm afraid you'll be with us for at least two weeks. And that's if everything goes all right."

"Well, I'll see about that. This isn't the first time I've been wounded. And I never spent any two weeks lying around. I heal faster on my feet. I'll do my lying around when they put me in the ground."

"Well, Mr. Moran, if you don't take it easy you might just get that rest sooner than you think. We'll take it day by day and see what happens."

"I guarantee I don't make any two weeks. Jane would miss me too much. She probably can't live without me."

"I see you've got your sense of humor back. I think you have that backwards. It's you who needs me to keep you in line. I'm the best thing that ever happened to you. Ha! Ha!"

The chief clears his throat and says, "I think it's getting a little deep in here. Rob, you and I had better get going. Some of us have work to do. Someone has to pick up the slack with hero boy here taking a vacation."

"What do you mean vacation? I only went to work with you temporarily to help solve the murders. I've done my part and plan to retire again. Working for you was cutting into my fishing career."

"We'll talk about this later, Duke. You enjoy your time off. Like you said you don't like to just sit around. And I'm sure that Jane doesn't want you around twenty-four hours a day. A person can take only so much of you."

The chief and Rob are chuckling as they leave the room. Even I'm laughing along with everyone else.

Jane says she has to get going and will be back later in the day. Which is probably a good thing, as the pain meds are starting to wear off. She gives me a kiss and leaves the room. Then nurse Nan asks if I need anything.

"Yes, I could use some more of whatever pain medication you gave me."

"Let me check with the doctor to see what I can give you. Eventually we'll have to wean you off of it. I'll be back shortly, so don't run away."

Chapter 25

. . . .

Wednesday July 5

I wake up with the sun shining in my face. Looking at the clock, I see its seven thirty in the morning. I'm so sick of this bed and the whole room. I push my call button for the nurse and wait for her to show. I've already checked the room out days before for my clothes. There's none here anywhere. If I have to, I'm going to leave the hospital today with the robe I have on. I don't care if my ass is hanging out.

"Finally," I say as nurse Nan enters the room. To my surprise she's carrying a stack of clothes. "I hope those are for me. I've had enough of this place to last me a lifetime. Nothing against you, of course. You've been great and I'll definitely miss you. But I feel great and I feel like I'm locked in prison."

"Yes, these are for you. The doctor will be in shortly for your final exam. Then he'll make out your discharge papers. I called Jane to tell her we were discharging you. She told me that her floral shop had a big order to deliver for a funeral today. Her helper Sandy called in sick today. So I told her that I'd come in and give you a ride home since it's my day off. I hope you don't mind that."

"No, I don't mind. I'm sorry to put you out like that though. I'm sure there are things you'd rather do than put up with me."

"I don't mind at all, Duke. We've spent a lot of time together this last week and a half. I feel like we're old friends."

"Okay, then let's get that damn doctor in here so we can fly the coop."

171

"Well, here he is now, Duke. I'll go get the car around to the front door and wait for you there."

The doctor does a quick exam of me and says he's amazed at how quickly I've mended. He tells me to hold off lifting anything over twenty pounds for the next week and then gradually increase it. "I also want to see you back here in a week for a recheck."

About five minutes later, another nurse comes in with my paperwork and makes me get in a wheelchair. She claims it's hospital rules. So I do as told. I will do anything to get out of here.

We get to the front door, and Nan is there waiting for us. I get out of the wheelchair and thank the nurse for taking care of me. Nan tries to help me into the car, but I shake her off and get in myself. I've had enough of people helping me.

We make small talk on the way to my place. I find Nan very easy to talk to and definitely easy to look at. She's a very cute petite young lady. I guess her to be about twenty-five years old.

I ask Nan, "So is there a Mr. Wonderful in your life? I'm sure someone as smart and great-looking as you has to fight the men off. Don't get me wrong, I'm not getting fresh. I'm just making small talk. Asking questions has been my job most of my life."

"I don't mind your asking. Actually, I'm not seeing anyone at this time. Between work and my sick mother, I keep pretty busy."

We pull up to my house and it feels good to be home. We get out of the car and Nan follows me in the back door. It's good to see that there's no new broken glass. Nan follows me into the house, which I feel is kind of weird.

So to be friendly I ask if she would like something to drink.

"Yes, I would like that, Duke. Anything you might have is fine."

I look in the fridge and see a few bottles of Lienenkugels and some Coke in there.

"I have Lienenkugels beer or Coke. Or else there is water."

"I'd love beer. I'm more a beer girl than the hard stuff."

"A girl after my heart. Here you go, and I think I'll join you. I don't plan on driving today, so it should mix well with the pain pills. Ha! Ha!"

I took a seat on the couch and was surprised when Nan sat down next to me. I didn't know what she was expecting. I guess she noticed that I was a little uncomfortable.

She says, "Duke, I have a confession to make. I've spent a lot of time with you the last week and a half. There's something I've wanted to do that whole time."

She sets her beer down and puts a hand on the side of my face and brings her lips to mine. She kisses me, and I'm so shocked that I automatically kiss her back. It has been a while that I've had physical contact with a female.

We part and Nan says, "Duke, I've become very fond of you in the last week. I don't know how you feel, but I'm here for you if you want."

"Well, Nan this is kind of a surprise. I like you a lot and find myself very comfortable around you. I also find you very pretty and definitely very sexy. A man would have to be out of his mind to not want you."

With that said she moves over me and straddles my lap. I have to admit it's very tough to not love this. She kissed me with a very deep kiss. I know the beer and pain pills are not helping me stop this.

Then all of a sudden, Jane's face come's front and center to my mind. It takes all my will power to push Nan back.

"Nan, I'm sorry, but I have to stop this. I know I'm going to kick myself later. But I do love Jane and couldn't live with myself if we go any further. This is one of the hardest things I've had to do."

"Something is definitely hard, that's for sure. Why don't we just go upstairs and let me take care of that?"

"Oh, Nan, you really know how to hurt a guy. I have to say no and I just hope you can understand. It's not you. You are the perfect woman, and I probably won't get any sleep tonight thinking of you. But I could never face Jane again if we go further."

"Okay, Duke, I have to say that Jane is a very lucky lady. I wish I could find someone as great as you. If you ever feel you need me, just let me know. Even if you just need to talk. I don't want to scare you completely off."

"Thanks, Nan I'm glad you understand. Right now, I think I need to take a nap. I think the beer and pain pills are working. So I'll see you later."

My plan is to take a nap and then go down to the police station and see what's happening there.

I wake up a short while later to a phone ringing. I automatically think I'm back in the hospital. But as I look around, I see I'm on my couch in my own house. My head feels much clearer now. I look around for the phone that won't stop ringing. So I get up and the pain starts up again in my back. I get the phone off my end table and answer it.

It's Jane calling to see how I am. I tell her, "I was just taking a nap. I guess I'm not one hundred percent yet. I think the beer I had when I got home didn't mix well with the pain pills. I don't want to take another pain pill, so I think I'll just take some Tylenol."

"So did nurse Nan give you a ride home?"

"Yes, she did, although I would have rather seen you. But I realize that you're busy, and I'm probably not very good company anyways. I do plan on going down to the station to see what's happening. I think I can handle that all right."

"You make sure that you're okay before you try driving. I don't want to see you back in the hospital again. I have plans for the two of us. I thought I'd bring over a couple of steaks to grill out tonight. And we'll figure out dessert afterwards."

"I'm not going to let anything interfere with that. Just the thought of that makes me feel a whole lot better. Of course, I mean the steak."

"Ha! Ha! Maybe all you'll get is steak, then. I'm sure you can survive without any dessert."

"Now there goes my appetite. I'd get down on my knees and beg forgiveness if it didn't hurt so damn much. I'll let you get back to work, and I really hope to see you tonight."

It's two o'clock in the afternoon so I figure I'm good enough to drive. I do notice that someone must have cleaned my kitchen floor up. I don't see any blood or evidence of my fight with my attacker. And the broken glass from the back door had been cleaned up to.

I get to the police station without any problem. I walk in and everyone is surprised to see me. After all the welcome backs, I head into the chief's office. He's surprised to see me also.

"Well, Chief where are we on the case now? Are you going to be able to put JJ away for the rest of his life?"

"Have a seat, Duke and I'll fill you in. We definitely have him for attempted murder of you. That should at least get him five to ten years."

"The problem with the other killings is we don't have a lot of evidence against him. We found the cash in his safe at his home. But he claims he didn't put it there and that someone is setting him up."

"And we didn't find any fingerprints at either murder site or at your house. Also, we didn't find any bloody clothes when we searched his place. Also, we found no knives with blood residue on them."

"We did however find that he has a floor safe that's the same as those at both crime scenes. And it was not built into a floor. It was sitting on the floor in his shop. We figure he might have had it to practice safe cracking on."

"The money was found in a different safe he keeps in his office in the house. But that's just circumstantial evidence. He admits to buying the floor safe at an estate sale, but never got around to installing it."

"He doesn't have a very good alibi for any of the crimes. He claims to have been at his girlfriend's place both nights. But that's not an air tight alibi. I don't know if we have enough to get him for the killings. Everything points to him, but it's mostly circumstantial."

"I think we should have enough. He got the cash out of the secret room in my basement. The killer had to be the only one to know it was there. Plus, he had the same safe as the victims that he probably practiced on. He also had good reason to have access to case out the houses. He probably did rodent service in the houses at one time or another."

"That's all true, but what do you think his motive would have been? It's not a ton of money to kill someone so gruesomely. It would have been a lot easier to break in when they weren't home. It almost seemed personal the way they were killed."

"I have a theory on that, Chief. I'd like to sit down and have a shot at questioning him. If I'm right, I might get a confession out of him."

"Well, I'm up for anything that nails him to the wall. I want to make sure he can't get off on flimsy evidence. So let's set up an interview for the two of you. I'll set it up for hopefully tomorrow."

"Sounds good, Chief, just give me a call for a time. I'll be here with bells on."

I figured I had an hour or two to kill. So I decided to stop in at the courthouse and check out a couple of things.

Once in the courthouse, I went up to see Markum Dooley the register of deeds.

"Hello, Markum how's it going? Have you got time to check out something for me?"

"Sure, Duke I would be glad to help out. It's good to see you're up and around. It sounded like things got pretty hairy for you."

"Yes, it was too close for comfort but everything seems to be working out for the better. Remember when you checked on the history of my house. It was in foreclosure from John Jones's grandfather. Can you see if the house was foreclosed on by the Black Crow Bank?"

"Sure, let me get it on the computer here. Here we go. Yes, it was foreclosed on by Black Crow Bank."

"But you wouldn't know why it was being foreclosed on, would you?"

"It says here that Mr. Jones was six months in arrears for mortgage payments. So the bank called in the loan."

"That's what I kind of thought. Thanks for the info, Markum. Can you print that out for me?"

"Sure, Duke, it's no problem. I heard it was the mayor that tried to kill you. I'm guessing this has something to do with that."

"Yes, I think it might. We should know for sure by tomorrow hopefully. Thanks for the help, Markum."

I got home a few minutes before five o'clock, and Jane pulled in right behind me. She is looking fantastic. I'm undressing her with my eyes. There isn't much to undress from what I can see. I hope like hell that it's not that time of the month. I'm still kicking my butt for turning down Nan earlier in the day. But if I had ever done that, I'd never be able to look Jane in the face again.

I was once told by someone that it's not the idea of getting lucky with a woman. It's the good feeling that someone finds you attractive and is interested in you. True love is hard to come by. Jane and I embrace immediately and have a long, heated kiss. The last thing on my mind right now is a steak dinner. I think Jane is feeling the same.

Once we get in the house Jane says, "I thought I lost you after the stabbing. I don't want to ever feel that again."

There are actually tears in her eyes. I try to reassure her by hugging her and whispering in her ear that I don't plan on it happening again. I direct her to my couch and fill her in on my hunch about JJ.

I filled her in on most of what we knew while I was in the hospital. Now I told her why I think JJ did it all. When I'm finished, she is in shock that JJ could be that vindictive.

"Well, I'm not sure of all this, but hopefully I'll find out tomorrow when I interview him."

We spent the next hour and a half holding each other and even worked in some tender lovemaking a couple of times. It was the most intense lovemaking I've ever experienced. I think we have taken our relationship to a new level.

"Well, my dear, I think I could use some fuel in this body of mine. How about I start the grill? You can lay here and relax if you wish."

"No, I'll get up and help. You should be taking it easy. The night isn't over yet, big boy."

"That sounds like a challenge to me. I missed the fireworks for July Fourth last night but they're much better tonight. I might need to go back to the hospital to get some rest."

Chapter 26

. . . .

Thursday July 6

I'm awoken to the phone ringing. I look at the clock by my bed to see its eight fifteen. So, I grab the phone and answer. It's the chief. "Good morning, Duke. How are you feeling today?"

"I'm somewhat sore and stiff but overall much better. Did you get an interview set up with JJ?"

"Yes, I did. Can you be here by nine o'clock this morning?"

"Yes, I can make that. I'll grab a quick shower and be right there."

"Okay, I'll have hot coffee and donuts waiting for you. See you shortly."

I make it to the station a few minutes to nine. The chief informs me they're getting JJ brought up from the jail. So I have time to get some coffee and a donut. I see an officer walking JJ through the office and taking him in the interview slash stockroom, so I grab the chief and we head in there.

"Well, if it isn't the great Duke Moran in the flesh. I heard you had a little accident. It's too bad you survived. I would have loved to see that."

"I guess if I hadn't fallen on top of you, it would have been easier for you to see. I hope I didn't get too much blood on you."

"I don't know what you're talking about. You must have me confused with someone else."

"Don't worry we have enough on you to lock you away for the rest of your life. You were found lying underneath me with blood all over you. Plus, your fingerprints are on the knife. There's no way you can beat that."

"Now where's your lawyer? I understand you've been read your rights already. But we'll read them to you again."

"I know my rights and I don't need a stinking lawyer. They're as bad as you cops are. I'm innocent and don't know why I'm here."

"Okay, then, John. We will be recording this to protect you as well as us. I'll ask again if you want your lawyer here. This is for the record."

"No, I don't want a lawyer here. You're going to railroad me any way you can. So let's just get it over with."

"To start with where were you on the evening of Saturday June 8 and Saturday June 15?"

"How the hell can I remember that long ago? I was probably at home. I don't have much of a social life. People don't give me the respect they should. I do all I can for this town, and they still call me the bug man. So, I spend most of my off time at home."

"Well, we have enough evidence to take you to trial for the murders of the Anderson and Browning families. We have the cash that was stolen out of their safes. It was found in your office safe. You have a white van, which was reported in the areas of the crimes."

"Plus, you just happen to have a floor safe the same exact model as the ones that were broken into. I figure you used that one to practice on so you could break into the other two. Actually, it was three that were broken into."

"I can't figure why you broke into the first two while the people were home and then killed them. It would have been much easier to do it when they weren't home."

"The third break in was when the people weren't home. There had to be some reason for that. Maybe you could enlighten me, John."

"You can go to hell, Moran. Or maybe I should call you moron like you are. If you had a brain, you'd be dangerous."

"I'm the moron, but you're the one facing the rest of your life in prison. If there was a death sentence in Wisconsin, you'd get it."

"I think I know why you killed the Andersons and the Browning's. They each had, what you think was, a hand in your family's problems over the years."

"As I was saying, John, I think your family's first problems started with Ed Browning. He was the only insurance agent around this whole area back in the day. I remember because my dad complained that he didn't have much choice in what insurance to get. The town was too small to have more than one insurance agent."

"Browning also did investment planning for people. He would take their money and invest it in different things for people. I'm guessing that your grandfather probably had money invested with him and somehow it all was lost in some investment deal. I'm only guessing because he couldn't come up with the money to keep the house. I suppose you blame Ed Browning for that."

"You're damn straight I blame him. My grandpa says that Browning claimed the market took a nose dive back then and a lot of people lost their money. But the truth was that Browning stole the money. Grandpa says Browning gave him some complicated story about what happened."

"It was damned funny, though that Browning just happened to but a new car at that time. He also put an addition on his house at the same time. Grandpa wasn't the only one that lost all his money. There were several other people that lost their life savings too.

"The man was a crook and ruined a lot of people's lives around here. He finally had to leave town because nobody wanted to do business with him. He deserved to die."

"So you're saying you took care of that for everyone?"

"No, I'm not saying I killed him. I'm just saying he deserved it."

"So are you saying his wife deserved it as well?"

"I'm sure she knew what he was doing all along. Any woman that stays with a man like that deserves the same."

"What about George and Anna Anderson. What did they ever do to you?

"That thief stole our home. Our family banked there for all their lives. Anderson wouldn't even work with my grandpa to help him. Grandpa missed three or four payments and Anderson started repossession proceedings on him right away. They had a big brawl over that and my grandpa ended up being arrested."

"You know you're bringing this all up is pissing me off Moran. You're as bad as the rest of them."

"Maybe you can enlighten us as to who's body that is in the basement. My guess would be your grandpa. How could you leave a family member just lying around dead in the basement like that without a proper burial? I thought you were a better person than that. Of course, the way you brutally murdered those people is unbelievable. I'm afraid you're going to spend the rest of your life in a ten by ten cage."

"I can't believe you'd kill those people for those lame reasons. That all happened years ago. You had to have more of a motive than that."

"What do you know, Moran? We weren't all born with a silver spoon in our mouths like you. Some of us have had to work for a living. When you bought our old house and started sticking money into it, I couldn't take that."

"Grandpa is at rest there. I tried to get him to go after that banker back then. We had a big fight over it, and he slugged me. He thought he knocked me out, but he hadn't. I grabbed a butcher knife from the kitchen and fixed his ass. I couldn't call an ambulance or the police without getting arrested so I remembered the room in the basement. It's pretty well sealed, so I put him down there and bought a bunch of lime to keep him from stinking."

"His social security checks kept coming so I cashed them in Black River whenever I went over there. After about a year a letter came from social security to check his status. I wrote back that he moved to California and didn't leave an address. That's the last I heard from them and the checks quit coming."

There's a knock at the door and the dispatcher sticks her head in and tells the chief he has an urgent call. "It's your son Rick with something important to tell you. He says it can't wait."

So the chief leaves the room and I'm alone with Jones.

"I have one question, John. What does the broken glass in the doors stand for? It's broken from the inside out. That makes no sense what so ever."

"That really bugs you, doesn't it? I think I'll just let it keep on bugging you. Maybe someday you'll figure it out."

"Everyone has always had it in for our family. This whole town has always been against us. It was only a matter of time before I got screwed over."

"What do you mean, John? You've always gotten along with everyone in town. Hell, we even voted you mayor. We wouldn't do that for someone we didn't like."

"That's just an honorary title. It doesn't have any power behind it. I'm basically a figurehead for the town. And it sure as hell doesn't pay anything. I have no retirement to fall back on. But I plan on having something now to retire on."

"I take it that your friends with Jack Knowles? His name came up in our investigation."

"Yeah I know that slime ball. I went to school with him. He's nothing but a drug dealing coke head. He's the one you should pin these murders on. No one will ever miss him in this lifetime. Of course, that might be kind of tough seeing how he's went to his maker already. Ha! Ha!"

"It's funny you should mention that. Mr. Knowles demise has not been announced as of yet. How would you know about that? It's also funny how he was stabbed several times just like the Andersons and Browning's."

"John I'm afraid your days of freedom are over. I'd suggest you get a good lawyer and try for some plea agreement. We have too much evidence against you."

"I'm not done yet, Moran. But you won't be around to see any of it."

All of a sudden, JJ lifts the table on his side and heaves it at me. At the same time, I see something in his hands even though his hands are handcuffed together. He leaps over the table as it falls on me and sticks something into my left shoulder. It's a knife of some kind.

My right arm is free, but I have limited movement with it because the table in on me. As I try to punch at him, he pulls the object out of my shoulder. He then goes to stab me again.

Next thing I hear is a loud shot. It's deafening in that small room. Something warm sprays over my head and there's a strong copper smell in the air.

John Jones goes limp and I feel additional weight on me.

I feel myself starting to black out. I can barely see someone pulling John's body off the table and then removing the table.

The next thing I realize is I'm waking up to a bright light again with two beautiful faces looking down on me. I feel like I'm in that movie call *Groundhog Day*.

The first voice I heard said, "We have to quit meeting like this. Do you think this is your private hotel or something?"

I recognize it as Nan's voice. And I also see Jane standing next to her. I can see that Jane has been crying.

"Jane, please stop crying. I didn't see this happening again to me, especially to happen right in the police station. I think this should be the end of my being a pin cushion for Mr. Jones. I heard a shot just before I passed out. I'm hoping he's dead."

My humor didn't seem to work on her. Nan left the room and Jane came over and gave me a nice big kiss. Then she said, "If you ever do this to me again, it will be the last time because I'll finish the job myself. I can't take all this tension about whether you'll live or die."

"I have no plans to do any more police work. I was just hired to work this one case. Now I can get back to my nice boring peaceful life."

The chief and Rob pick this time to come into the room and the first thing I say is that I quit. "I don't have nine lives like a cat. So where do we stand on the John Jones case?"

"Well, first let me say how sorry I am about what happened to you, Duke. I never should have left you alone in that room. Somehow, he got a butter knife from the cafeteria. I think someone snuck it in to him. He then sharpened it on the rough brick wall of his cell. We found the areas where he scraped it. He had gotten it sharp enough that you could cut paper with it."

"Somehow he had it stuck in the elastic of his jail sweats. I don't know how he did it because those sweats are pretty loose."

"Anyways you got lucky because the doctor said a couple more inches over and he would have got you in the heart. I know you don't feel very lucky and I sincerely apologize."

"You'll be glad to hear that Mr. Jones didn't make it. I made it back to the room just as he was getting ready to stab you again. I've never had to shoot someone like that. Once this is all cleaned up, I plan on retiring."

"I took this job thinking it would be a nice easy way to finish up before retirement. We're going to need a new mayor, so I think I'll run for that job. It's got to be a lot easier than this one."

"Hey, Duke I think you should run for the police chief job. You would be perfect for it. This was not the normal way things go on this job here. You could have Rob as your assistant. That way he could learn more about the job and you would have plenty of time to work on your house or fish. It's something to think about."

"I don't know about that. I believe Jane here might have something to say about that. But that's a story for another day.

"Mr. Moran, if you even think about taking that job, I'll be sharpening up my knives. I don't want to be up nights worrying about my husband."

The End